A YANKEE GIRL AT SHILOH

By

Alice Turner Curtis

(Originally Published in 1922)

Table of Contents

Introduction

Mrs. Curtis in the two other books of this set, "A Yankee Girl at Fort Sumter" and "A Yankee Girl at Bull Run," has told delightful stories of little Northern heroines at these great battles.

In this present story Berenice Arnold with her mother and father came from Vermont to the mountains of Tennessee in order that Mr. Arnold might regain his health. During the second winter of their stay the Armies of the North and the South began to draw closer to Shiloh, which was not far from the Arnold cabin. Berry had many exciting adventures. She found a young runaway slave-girl, who was sheltered by her parents and proved a devoted friend. She was mistaken for a boy by a Southern spy because of the fact that she wore blue corduroy knickerbockers. He tried to force her to bear secret messages to his Commander, but Berry, braving his anger and the misunderstandings in the Northern camp, managed to give military information to the Northern Army, which enabled it to gain a complete victory. Her deed was so splendid that General Grant himself visited the Arnold cabin to dine with Berry and thank her personally.

Alice Turner Curtis

CHAPTER I
"BERRY"

There had been a light fall of snow during the night, and the tall oak trees that grew near the Arnolds' log cabin, which stood on the slope of a wooded ridge overlooking the Tennessee River, were still sprinkled with clinging white flakes when the heavy door of the cabin was pushed open and a slender little figure appeared on the rough porch.

If a stranger had been passing along the trail that led near this secluded cabin he would perhaps have decided that it was a boy who darted out and jumped up and down exclaiming, "Snow! Snow! Just like Vermont snow!" for the curling brown hair was cut short, and the blue flannel blouse, the baggy knickerbockers of blue corduroy, as well as the stout leather shoes, were all in keeping as a suitable costume for a ten-year-old lad whose home was a log cabin in the rough region on the westerly bank of the Tennessee River, over two hundred miles from its mouth. And when some casual stranger, failing to see the blue corduroys, so mistook Berenice Arnold, and called her "my lad," she was very well pleased.

On this January morning, in 1862, Berenice had been awakened at an unusually early hour by a call from her father, telling her to dress quickly and hasten down in time to see the snow, that lay like a white veil over the wooded slopes, before the sun came out from behind the distant mountains and swept it away.

"Snow! Berry! Not enough for a sleigh ride, but enough to make you think of Vermont," he had called, as if announcing an unexpected delight. For the Arnolds had only lived in Tennessee for two years. Berry was nine years old when, with her father and mother and her older brother Francis, she had left the big white house in the pleasant Vermont village near Montpelier and come to this hillside cabin where Mr. Arnold hoped to regain something of his former health and strength. This was the second winter, and this fall of snow in early January was the first real snowfall since their arrival. There had been many "flurries," but, until this January morning, not enough had fallen to whiten wood and trail; and the Arnolds ran to door and windows exclaiming over the new beauty of the slopes and forest beneath their white coverlets.

"What would Francis say to this?" exclaimed Berry, as her father came out and stood beside her.

Francis was now a soldier, with the Northern forces in Virginia, and Berry's thoughts were often with her brother; wondering why he had been so determined, a year ago, to return to Vermont and enlist in a Northern regiment in the conflict to prevent the Southern States from leaving the Union, and to bring an end to the slavery of the negroes in America. Francis had been only eighteen when he had become a soldier, and Berry knew that her father and mother had both been willing that he should go. The little girl had often puzzled about it, for she had heard her father say that when Abraham Lincoln became President the United States would soon understand each other and all the talk of war would come to an end. But even Mr. Lincoln had not been able to avert the conflict; and the hillside cabin, ten miles distant from the flourishing town of Corinth, was shadowed by the news of far-off battles.

"You must write Francis about it," responded Berry's father; "tell him the slope is as white as the main street at home in Vermont in midwinter." And Berry nodded smilingly.

"It will be gone before noon, so we can go out to the river road, and see what the mail-rider left for us yesterday," continued Mr. Arnold.

"And, if 'tis not too muddy, can we not walk as far as Lick Creek and try for fish?" asked Berry, her brown eyes shining with eagerness at the thought of a long tramp with her father through the winter woods, and, best of all, the fun of catching a pickerel or bass from the waters of Lick Creek. For, in the two years that Berry had lived on this remote mountain slope, she had been her father's constant companion in his out-of-door life, and it was for that reason that her mother had decided to dress the little girl in suitable clothing. If Berry had been obliged to wear dainty clothes, if her hair had been long and hung down her back in curls or braids, and her feet covered only by thin kid shoes, she would never have known every nook and crevice along the table-land, rolling and ridgy, a few miles above Pittsburg Landing, a place that was to become an historic spot.

"No fishing to-day," her father declared; and, as at that moment Mrs. Arnold called them to breakfast, he did not add that he intended going in the opposite direction that morning to visit the rude log chapel known as Shiloh church, where Sunday services were occasionally held, and where Mr. Arnold now and then busied himself in repairing windows, painting the outer door, and doing such light work as his strength was equal to, in improving the condition of the neglected building. Berry was of great assistance to her father in this work; he had taught her how to use a plane, and smooth off a piece of wood until it was fit for use. She knew the names and use of all the tools he used about his carpentering work; and as a trip to Shiloh church meant a picnic dinner cooked in the open air, Berry was always well pleased when her father set off in that direction; and on hearing that he intended to start as soon as the sun was well up she quite forgot her plan to visit Lick Creek.

Berry helped her mother clear the table and wash the dishes while her father selected the few tools he would need, and also packed a small basket with food for their midday meal; and when he called "All ready for the trail," Berry slipped on her brown corduroy jacket and her knitted cap of scarlet wool and was ready to start.

"If there is a letter from Francis in the mail-box I will bring it home as fast as I can, Mother," she promised, as Mrs. Arnold stood on the porch to watch them start.

"We will be home before sunset," Mr. Arnold promised, and followed Berry, who was running down the trail.

Mrs. Arnold stood looking after them for a moment, smiling at Berry's delight in starting off for a day in the woods, and thinking gratefully of her husband's improvement in health. Their cabin was several miles from any neighbors, and Mrs. Arnold had in the first months of their stay often been homesick for the friends and home she had left so far away among the peaceful hills of Vermont. But gradually the peace and quiet of their simple life in the hillside cabin, Berry's happiness in playing out-of-doors, and, best of all, the improvement in Mr. Arnold's health, reconciled her to the exile from New England. Often she accompanied her husband and Berry on their excursions, but this morning she intended writing a long letter to her soldier son.

Before Berry and her father reached the mail-box, that was fastened to a stout oak tree on the highway, the veil of snow had nearly disappeared, and the piles of brown leaves along the trail glistened in the morning sun. There was nothing in the box, and Mr. Arnold and Berry turned back into a path that would lead them direct to Shiloh church. A flock of bluejays started up from the underbrush and went scolding and screaming into the branches of a tall chestnut tree, their blue feathers and crested heads catching the sunlight and brightening the shadowy path. Berry gazed after them wonderingly. "I do think it's a pity they squawk so," she said thoughtfully, "when they are so lovely to look at. And the mocking-birds are so plain and gray."

Berry had become familiar with the birds who nested near the woodland cabin, and had learned much about their ways. She knew that the handsome jay was a thief who ate the eggs from the nests of other birds and sometimes even destroyed the birds. She knew where the fine cardinal in his scarlet coat, and Madam Cardinal in her more modest colors, made their nest in the underbrush along the banks of the ravine; and the tiny wrens who fluttered about the trail were her friends. But, best of all, Berry loved the mocking-birds, with their musical trills and clear song. Even in January they could be heard near the cabin; not with their springtime song, but with soft notes and hopeful calls. The little girl often put bits of bread and cake on the porch rail, and it was not long before the birds had discovered this unexpected bounty and came fluttering down to look for it; and gradually the family had all made friends among their bird neighbors, giving them names, and keeping a sharp outlook for the young birds who were their springtime visitors.

"What are you going to do to-day, Father?" Berry questioned as they came in sight of the log building that stood on the crest of the ridge.

"I am going to fix the benches. Some of them are dropping to pieces," responded her father. "I have a good store of fine oak wood dry and ready for use in the shed near the church, and we can soon make the old seats as good as new."

"And may I put the new rail on the pulpit? I have polished it until it shines like glass," said Berry, as they came out into the little clearing in which the church stood.

"Of course," her father agreed, smiling down at his little daughter's eager face. He was well pleased that Berry found pleasure in the outdoor life, that she was learning to do many things that little girls seldom have an opportunity to learn, and that she was as active and healthy as it was possible for a girl to be.

Before beginning the work he had planned Mr. Arnold stood looking at the wild country spread out before him. "Look, Berry," he said, pointing to a ravine on the left, along which ran the main road to Corinth. "This spot is like a picture in a frame," he continued, "the little streams of Owl Creek and Lick Creek, the road to Corinth, and the Tennessee River making the frame. It would make a safe camp for an army," he added thoughtfully, but without an idea that within three months that very spot would be the scene of one of the most important battles of the Civil War; or that his little daughter who stood so quietly beside him would, by her courage and endurance, have rendered a great service to the cause of the Northern forces.

They had walked a long distance, and seated themselves on the broad step of the chapel for a rest.

"It is nearly noon; I'll start our fire and get lunch under way," said Mr. Arnold. But Berry was eager to do this; for she knew exactly how to lay a fire in the open; how to bake potatoes in hot ashes, and to broil bacon over the coals; and to set the tin pail, in which they made coffee, where it would boil slowly.

"All right," agreed Mr. Arnold, "I'll fetch the wood."

Berry ran along the ridge to where a granite ledge made a good shelter for a blaze, and in a short time a little curl of smoke crept into the air, and the appetizing odor of broiling bacon and of fragrant coffee made Mr. Arnold declare that he was "hungry as a bear," greatly to Berry's delight.

"Wouldn't it be splendid if Francis was here?" she said, as she and her father began their luncheon.

"Not much hope of seeing Francis this winter," replied Mr. Arnold.

"I hate war!" Berry declared, breaking open a well-baked potato, and proceeding to sprinkle salt on it. "If it were not for war Francis would be here this minute."

"No; Francis would be in college," her father rejoined.

"What's college?" Berry demanded.

"Why, Berenice Isabel Arnold!" exclaimed her father in amazement. "I will have to turn schoolmaster and keep you shut in the house with books if you really do not know the meaning of 'college'!"

Berry shook her head: her mouth was filled with hot potato, and she could not speak.

"College is a school where young men like Francis learn more important things than can be taught to younger boys," explained her father. "And I have made up my mind, Berry; to-morrow your regular lessons begin."

"Oh, Father! Not like the school at home?" Berry pleaded. "Not geography and maps, and arithmetic and sums, and grammar and compositions?"

"Exactly! It will never do for a little Yankee girl, even if she does live in Tennessee, to grow up without an education. School will begin to-morrow!" replied Mr. Arnold.

"Then Mollie Bragg will have to go to school with me," Berry declared.

CHAPTER II
MOLLIE BRAGG

The nearest neighbors to the Arnolds were a family named Bragg, who lived in a cabin some three miles distant, near the road leading to Corinth. The Braggs' cabin was not a comfortable, convenient home such as the Arnolds had made their own mountain cabin. The doors of the Braggs' cabin sagged from clumsy leather hinges; the floor of the rough porch was broken here and there, so that anyone entering the house had to be careful where he stepped. Mr. Bragg announced each day that he was "gwine ter try mighty hard to find time to fix that po'ch, an' mend up the roof." But days, weeks, and months went by and no repairs were made, although Mr. Bragg spent long hours on the porch, tilted back against the house in an old chair, smoking, and, as he would promptly explain to any visitor, "tryin' to rest up."

Indoors Mrs. Bragg swept and scoured, mended the poor garments of her family, and tried her best to make the rough place pleasant for her children. Mollie Bragg, the youngest of the family, was a little girl about the age of Berenice Arnold, but not as tall or strongly built as Berry. Mollie's eyes were a pale blue, her hair, which hung straight about her thin little face, was a pale yellow, and her arms and legs were so thin that Berry sometimes wondered that they did not break as Mollie ran down the rough mountain paths, or valiantly followed Berry in climbing a tall tree to peer into the nest of a robin or yellowhammer. Mollie's elder sister had left home, the year the Arnolds came to Tennessee, to live with an aunt in Nashville, and the only son, a lad of sixteen, had run away to join the army of the Confederacy, so that in January, 1862, Mollie was the only child at home.

Although the Arnold and Bragg cabins were three miles apart, hardly a day passed that Mollie and Berry did not see each other. Mollie would often set out early in the morning and appear at the Arnolds' door before they had finished breakfast, to be eagerly welcomed by Berry, and urged to a seat at the round breakfast table near the big window that overlooked the ravine by Mrs. Arnold, and helped to the well-cooked porridge, followed by crisp bacon and toast, and often a dish of stewed fruit, all of which the little visitor evidently enjoyed.

To Mollie the Arnolds' cabin seemed the finest place in the world. Although it had only five rooms, and the family had their meals in the kitchen, it was indeed a pleasant and attractive home, with its muslin-curtained windows, its floors painted a shining yellow, with rag rugs here and there, the open fire in the sitting-room that blazed so cheerfully on winter days, the well-filled bookshelves in one corner and the stout wooden chairs and settles with their big feather-filled cushions. Mr. Arnold had spent a good part of his time in improving the cabin from the rough state in which they had found it, and had made most of the simple furniture. A vine-covered fence enclosed the yard, where Berry had her own garden. Each spring she began by planting lettuce and radishes, and then peas and carrots and string beans; before these had time to sprout she had bordered her vegetable beds with spring flowers. Mollie learned many things from her new friends, and, in her turn, showed Berry where the wild trillium and Jack-in-the-pulpit could be found, and where to look for the nests of cardinal and mocking-bird, birds that the little Yankee girl had never seen before coming to Tennessee. Therefore when Mr. Arnold declared that it was time for Berry to have regular lessons, "to begin school," as he termed it, it was quite natural for Berry to say that Mollie Bragg would also have to study.

There was no schoolhouse within miles of these mountain cabins where the little girls could "begin school," and Berry understood that her father would be her teacher. And on the day after their excursion to Shiloh church

Mr. Arnold told Berry that she could go to the Braggs' cabin and ask Mollie to be her schoolmate.

"Tell her school begins at ten o'clock each morning and closes at twelve," he said as Berry put on her cap and started toward the door.

"And say to Mrs. Bragg that we shall expect Mollie to stay for dinner," added Mrs. Arnold, who realized that the Bragg family seldom had the kind of food that would nourish a delicate child like Mollie, and welcomed the opportunity to give her small neighbor one good meal each day.

"All right," Berry called back, as she ran down the path, turning to wave her hand before the thick growing forest trees hid her from sight.

Berry's way led through the forest, across a wide brook that went dancing down over its rocky bed toward the river, and then the path turned into the highway near which was the rough clearing surrounding the Braggs' cabin. A tiny gray bird called "Chick-a-dee-dee-dee," as if to greet the red-capped little figure that ran so swiftly along the rough path. Further on she heard the cheerful whistle of the cardinal, and stopped for a moment to look up into the wide-spreading branches of the big trees that towered above her, hoping for a glimpse of the red-coated songster, but he was not to be seen.

The crossing of the wide brook meant stepping carefully from stone to stone until the middle of the stream was reached, where a broad flat rock gave a firm foothold, and from which Berry was accustomed to jump to the opposite bank. She made the passage skilfully, springing over the rushing water and landing on firm ground with the lightness and sure footing of an active boy; before she had taken a further step, however, a chuckling voice close at hand called: "Well done, youngster! It takes a Tennessee lad to jump," and Berry found herself facing a tall man whose face was nearly covered by a brown beard, and whose brown eyes twinkled with amusement at her surprise. He wore a round, close-fitting cap of coonskin, a leather jacket, with stout trousers of corduroy and high boots. A hunter's belt held a revolver and hunting-knife, and a knapsack was strapped across his shoulders. It was seldom that Berry encountered anyone in her forest tramps, but she had been taught to believe in the friendliness of the mountain people, and smiled and nodded in response to the man's greeting.

"I can jump farther than that," she boasted. "I can jump farther than most boys of my age."

The man nodded approvingly. "Well, you ain't so stocky as some," he said thoughtfully. "Guess your ma kind of likes to dress you up, don't she, sonny?" he continued, with an amused glance at Berry's red silk tie and scarlet wool cap.

Berry nodded. If this stranger mistook her for a boy she did not mean to undeceive him.

"Well," continued the man, "you can't help that, my lad. What's your name?"

"Berry," responded the little girl.

"Berry what?" he continued.

"Berenice," said Berry, thinking that now the stranger had discovered her secret, and that he would at once tell her that the place for little girls was at home, helping their mother, as Mr. Bragg so often announced.

But the man evidently had not understood her. "'Nees,' eh! Berry Nees. Well, you mountain folks have queer names. But I'm glad to make your acquaintance. I reckon you can run considerable as well as jump?"

"Yes," Berry replied quickly, well pleased that she need not hear that "Girls should not be running wild in boys' clothes," as had sometimes been said to her. "I can run faster than Len Bragg, who is sixteen years old."

"Where does Len Bragg live?" questioned the man.

"Oh! He's in the war! He's with General Johnston's army," replied Berry promptly.

"That's right!" declared the man approvingly. "There's not a finer man in the Confederate army than Albert Sidney Johnston."

Berry had heard her own father praise General Johnston's character, so she was not surprised, and replied politely, "Yes, sir."

"I'm bound for Corinth myself," continued the man. "I've journeyed across country from Fort Donelson, and I reckon I shan't stop long at Corinth; like as not I may come back this way, long in the spring," and the man smiled to himself as if well pleased with such a prospect. "If I do, Berry, maybe I'll want you to let me see if you can run as fast as you say. Maybe I'll want you to take a message to Pittsburg Landing in a hurry for me." And the man's eyes rested sharply upon Berry.

Before Berry could reply the man spoke again, and in a sharper tone than he had yet used.

"And see here, my lad! Don't you let on to a living soul about having met me. Understand?" and his hand touched the sheath of his hunting-knife in a threatening manner. But Berry did not wait to answer; she was off like a flash, not keeping to the path, but darting behind big trees, circling around underbrush and at last hiding behind a tall stump. She heard the man crashing along behind her, but Berry's boast of being a swift runner was well proved; the woodsman could not overtake her. Berry smiled to herself as she heard him floundering about through the thickets. She was not at all afraid of being caught, for she knew all the forest ways, and many a hiding-place. She kept very quiet, however, and did not venture out from behind the stump until a hovering flock of nuthatches, who had been scolding vigorously at being disturbed, settled down in a near-by thicket.

"He's gone," she whispered, and stepped cautiously out; "he didn't come this way or the nuthatches would not have stopped flying."

Berry peered sharply about, however, as she made her way noiselessly from tree to tree, stopping often to listen for any sound that might mean she was being followed, but, except for the far-off call of woodland birds, the forest was quiet. Berry was sure the man had given up trying to find her, and hastened down the ridge to the Braggs' cabin. She said nothing of her adventure to the Braggs, but told of her father's plan for morning lessons. "Mollie may come every day, may she not?" she pleaded; "and Mother wants her to stay for dinners."

Mrs. Bragg's anxious face had brightened as Berry spoke of lessons, and she answered quickly, "I reckon prayers are answered, fer I've been a hopin' and a prayin' there'd be some chance for Mollie to get book-larnin', but no way seemed to open, and now your folks come along an' want to teach her. Of course she can come, an' mighty thankful fer the chanst," and Mrs. Bragg wiped her faded eyes with the corner of her worn apron, and managed to smile at Mollie, who was jumping up and down as if too happy to keep still. Mr. Bragg had started off to look after the traps he set along the river banks for muskrats, whose skins he sold to a trader in Corinth, so there was no argument about the "foolishness of book-larnin'," for Mr. Bragg often proudly announced that he "never had no schoolin', an' never was any the wus' fer it," without any idea that his poverty and laziness had been caused by his ignorance.

"School begins to-morrow," Berry added, "at ten o'clock."

"What will we learn to-morrow?" Mollie asked eagerly, her pale blue eyes shining with delight.

Berry shook her head. "I don't know. I expect it will be a surprise. I don't believe it will be like a real school," she replied.

Mollie's smile vanished. To go to a "real school" seemed the finest thing in the world to the little mountain girl, who had not even known the letters of the alphabet until Berry had taught them to her, and who could now, at ten years of age, only read words of one syllable, and was just beginning to learn the meaning of figures.

Berry was quick to notice the change in Mollie's expression, and added, "I mean we won't sit behind little desks, and keep as quiet as mice, the way girls do in schools."

"P'raps we will," Mollie rejoined hopefully; "p'raps I'll learn writin'."

"Of course you will," Berry declared, and Mollie's smile promptly reappeared.

"May I spin this morning?" Berry asked, going toward the big spinning-wheel that stood in one corner of the kitchen, on which Mrs. Bragg spun the yarn for the stockings worn by the family, and often permitted Berry to spin the soft fleecy rolls of wool into yarn. Berry always considered this permission a great privilege, and her father had promised to make a spinning-wheel for her.

Usually Mrs. Bragg was quite ready to let Berry try her hand at the wheel, but this morning she shook her head dolefully.

"The wheel's give out," she declared. "Steve promised to take a look at it, but land knows when he'll get 'round to it."

Berry approached the big wheel and looked at it anxiously. "What's the matter with it?" she asked.

"'Twon't move!" and to prove this Mrs. Bragg touched the rim of the wheel, that usually responded to the lightest touch, but now kept firm and steady.

Berry had watched her father in his work with tools, had seen him oil hinges that would not move, or loosen nuts that held some wheel or bar too tightly, and she had been taught to do many things that most little girls never learn; so now she examined the wheel with so serious a face that Mrs. Bragg looked at her in amazement.

"If I had a screw-driver and an oil-can I believe I could fix it," she declared.

"Fer the land's sake!" muttered Mrs. Bragg. "We never saw a screw-driver, but there's a broken knife that'll twist a screw mighty fine."

"Perhaps that would do," Berry responded gravely, and Mollie ran off to find the broken knife, while Berry peered under the wheel-bench to make sure that she understood the simple movement of the wheel.

Mrs. Bragg watched Berry as the little girl carefully loosened and adjusted the axle on which the wheel turned, until it would move, but it did not move smoothly.

"It needs a drop of oil!" Berry announced.

But the Bragg cabin could furnish nothing better than a bit of melted tallow, and Mrs. Bragg declared that far superior to oil, and hastened to prepare it, and at last, to the amazement and delight of Mrs. Bragg and Mollie, and to Berry's great satisfaction, the big wheel revolved as swiftly as ever.

"I reckon you know ter do sich things, Berry, on account of being a Yankee girl," Mrs. Bragg declared admiringly. "Steve says folks up North prides theirselves on workin', an' on inventin' ways ter make work. I declar' to it, I'll have ter rest a spell," and Mrs. Bragg sank down on a wooden bench near the door.

"Maw, tell Berry that story you tole me 'bout the selfish mouse," said Mollie. "Maw kin tell gran' stories, Berry," the little girl continued eagerly. "W'en we wus off up in the mountains she used ter tell a new one mos' every night."

Berry's face brightened at the prospect of a story, and Mrs. Bragg said she would tell it as nearly as she could remember it.

"It's 'bout a mouse that jes' was set on gettin' all he could fer hisself," she explained. "This mouse lived with his mother an' four brothers in a fine cabin whar thar was a big cupboard. Thar was cakes an' cheese an' nice white bread, an' cold meat; an', like as not, thar was raisins an' nuts in that thar cupboard. But the door was allers kep' shut tight, an' thar was a big white cat that, seemingly, was allers lurkin' roun' that pantry door. So Mother Mouse warned her children to be satisfied with the crumbs they could pick up 'roun' the kitchen. But one day one of the little mice found that the door was open and he slipped in, an' 'twa'n't a minute afore that little mouse found a big round cheese an' began to nibble it; an' he was so busy and so happy that he didn't hear the cupboard door shut, or notice that 'twas dark.

"Wal, Mother Mouse didn't miss him fer a considerable spell, bein' busy collectin' grain jest outside the cabin. But when it began ter get dark she calls fer the young ones so's to settle down fer the night, an' she finds one of 'em don' come. The first thing Mother Mouse thought of was the white cat, but the cat wasn't anywhar ter be seen; so Mother Mouse goes all about the kitchen calling the missing mouse, an' when she crept by the cupboard she heard a little bit of a squeak, and then she stopped mighty quick. She knew the little mouse was in that cupboard, an' she prob'ly knew that thar war traps set in it. So she calls her fam'ly an' then says she, 'Your brother is in thar, an' we mus' get him out. Now the folks have all gone to bed, an' we'll begin work.' So she began to nibble at the edge of the door, and the little mice did their best to help her, and jes' 'fore daylight there was a hole big enough for the little mouse to come through. But he wouldn't come. Says he, 'I only squeaked so you'd know that I'm well fixed fer life,' says he. 'I ain' no need ever to gather kitchen crumbs again,' he says, 'an' so you can all go your ways an' ferget me.' An' he ran back to his cheese. Wal, at that very minute the woman of the house came into the kitchen to light up the fire, an' she sees the mice. 'My land!' she calls out; an' off went Mother Mouse and all her family into a safe hiding-place. But the woman opened the cupboard door, and then she called, 'Puss, puss!' an' the big cat came running, an' into the pantry she sprung an' the little mouse, who had felt so grand and had scorned his own folks who were tryin' ter help him, was so stupid and clumsy because he had eaten so much that he couldn't run, and in a minute the cat had grabbed him and fetched him out to the kitchen an' ate him up. Thar," Mrs. Bragg concluded, "I guess I'll hev to stir up a corn pone fer dinner," and she got up from the bench.

"What became of the Mother Mouse and the other little mice?" Berry demanded.

But Mrs. Bragg shook her head, "I reckon they jes' moved away," she said.

It was now nearly noon, and Berry realized that she must get home as soon as possible; so reminding Mollie that "school" would begin the next morning, she bade them good-bye.

As soon as she had left the Bragg cabin Berry's thoughts flew back to the man she had encountered that morning. Although she had not spoken of him to Mrs. Bragg, for some reason that she could not easily account for, she was now eager to reach home and tell her father and mother of the stranger who had taken her for a boy, and who had threatened her.

"I'll go home another path," she decided. "I never want to see that man again," and she made her way up the crest of the ridge, circling about thick growths of trees and underbrush, and coming into the trail that led to the cabin a mile above the place where she had encountered the stranger.

CHAPTER III
SCHOOL

It was with a grave face that Mr. Arnold listened to Berry's story of her morning's adventure at the brook; and her mother instantly declared that Berry could no longer run about alone. "The man was probably a Confederate spy," she said anxiously, "and if he had discovered that a family from New England were living near by, that, instead of being a little boy of Tennessee, you were a little Yankee girl, we cannot tell what would have happened."

"Yes, I believe the man has been traveling along the Cumberland and Tennessee Rivers looking over the Confederate line of defense, and his saying he might return this way in the spring may mean that the Confederates fear an attack will be made upon Fort Henry or Fort Donelson. If the Union army could capture these forts and open the Tennessee and Cumberland rivers, the Confederate line of defense would be destroyed," said Mr. Arnold thoughtfully; and Mrs. Arnold instantly added, "We surely need not fear any battle taking place near this remote spot, but with spies everywhere we must take all possible precautions. I hope you did not tell the Braggs of meeting a stranger, Berry?" she added.

"No; I didn't tell Mrs. Bragg. I don't know why I didn't," Berry responded thoughtfully. "I guess I was really frightened after all, and didn't want Mrs. Bragg to know it."

"Nonsense, Berry!" said Mr. Arnold sharply. "You could run away from anyone. And if you blew your whistle, even if you were too far away for me to hear and come to your assistance, it would make any dangerous person sure that help was close at hand, and would probably frighten him away."

Berry's father did not like the idea of the little girl going about in fear. He knew it would destroy all her pleasure in the free woodland life which they had all taken so much happiness in. The whistle of which he spoke had been a gift to Berry from her brother Francis. It was a silver whistle, attached to a long silver chain that Berry always wore about her neck, with the whistle tucked into the pocket of her blouse. During the first year in the cabin Mr. Arnold had not been sufficiently strong to walk far, and it was Francis who had chopped the wood for the cabin fires, journeyed to Corinth for necessary provisions, and fished for bass and pickerel along the river; and Berry had often been his companion. He had given her the whistle so if she lost sight of him in the woodland trails she could instantly call him; and Berry valued it more than anything else and never left the cabin without it.

Nothing more was said that day in regard to the stranger, but in the afternoon Mr. Arnold started off into the forest, telling Berry that he thought she would better stay and keep her mother company. He followed the trail to the Braggs' cabin, and made his way for some distance up the stream where Berry had encountered the stranger; but he found nothing to cause alarm, and was tempted to believe that, after all, the man might have been only a woodsman journeying across country, who had thought it an amusing game to frighten the small boy for whom he had mistaken Berry.

As he walked along the ridge and down the slope to his cabin Mr. Arnold thought to himself that, as his wife had said that noon, however the conflict went between the armies of the North and the South, there was small danger of its coming nearer to Shiloh church than the defensive line of the Confederates at the river forts, and which stretched on through Kentucky from the Mississippi River to the Cumberland Mountains. The control of this defense was in the hands of General Albert Sidney Johnston, a man respected alike by his opponents and his soldiers. His line of defense included Fort Henry, on the right bank of the Tennessee, and Fort

Donelson, on the left bank of the Cumberland River; and Mr. Arnold was confident that General Ulysses S. Grant, the commander of Union forces in the West, would not long delay in an attempt to conquer these river strongholds. "With those forts destroyed Grant's army could soon break the whole western line of defense," reflected Mr. Arnold, little realizing that within a month this very thing would be accomplished.

Before Mr. Arnold reached home the sky filled with heavy clouds and it began to snow. "Glad Berry is indoors," he thought, as he approached the cabin and saw the dancing blaze of the sitting-room fire shine out through the windows. Berry and her mother were on the settle beside the fire busy with sewing.

"It looks just like my things, only smaller," said Berry, holding up a blue serge blouse.

"Only Mollie's suit is a skirt and blouse, instead of knickerbockers," her mother smilingly reminded her.

"Well, Mollie would like knickerbockers, but her father never would let her wear them," said Berry. "Why does Mr. Bragg think I ought to wear long calico skirts, I wonder? I could not run or climb trees or jump across brooks if I wore skirts. Mollie is always tearing hers, and tumbling down when she runs after me."

"Mr. Bragg doesn't really think, my dear. He simply echoes," responded Mrs. Arnold. "But I am sure Mollie will like her new skirt."

"Won't she be surprised, Mother, to have a birthday party? And on the very day school begins. The minute Mrs. Bragg said that January tenth was Mollie's birthday I thought I'd make her a present; but it was you who thought of a party," and Berry gazed admiringly at her pretty, smiling mother, who was always thinking of such interesting things for little girls to do. For it was Mrs. Arnold who had suggested ripping up a blue serge skirt of her own and making a blouse and skirt of it for Mollie. But it was Berry who, with her mother's help, had cut out blouse and skirt, and who had stitched the seams and embroidered a star in red worsted on the corners of the collar.

When the Arnolds came to Tennessee they had brought a good store of clothing; but they had not believed a great war was so close at hand, a war that was to impoverish the Southern States and to make it nearly impossible for people to procure suitable clothing; and at the close of their second year in their mountain cabin the Arnolds began to realize that they must take good care of their garments, as they could not purchase new material in the town of Corinth. With the Braggs conditions were more difficult, as they had never possessed decent clothing; such dresses as Mrs. Bragg had managed to secure for herself and Mollie were worn to rags. Mrs. Arnold had given Mrs. Bragg a dress of stout gingham; but poor little Mollie ran about in a thin worn calico. Mrs. Arnold was teaching the little girl to knit a jacket for herself of the fine blue yarn that her mother spun, and, with a dress of serge, Mollie would soon be comfortably clothed.

When the last stitches were set and Mollie's dress was quite finished, Berry carried the serge blouse and skirt into her own room, which opened from the sitting-room, and that was as pleasant a chamber as any little girl could ask. The floor of the room, like all the cabin floors, was painted yellow. The walls and ceiling were boarded with pine, whose soft color blended with the floor. Mr. Arnold and Francis had built this room on to the cabin, and its wide window overlooked the deep ravine toward Lick Creek. But a tall oak tree grew so close to the cabin on this side as to hide the little building from sight, and when Berry looked from her window she looked out between the branches of the trees toward rough banks and wooded ridges. Mr. Arnold had made the simple white bedstead that stood in Berry's room, and the dressing-table, over which hung a small square mirror. And Francis had built the box-like window-seat, which Mrs. Arnold had covered with flowered chintz which she had brought with her from the North, and had made curtains for the window of the same material. A white rug of sheepskin lay beside the bed, and there was a chest of drawers in one corner of the room, and a small wooden rocking-chair painted white.

Berry put Mollie's new dress in the lower drawer of the wide chest and looked at it admiringly. Then, from a far corner of the drawer she took a long package wrapped in a piece of newspaper—for tissue and wrapping paper were not easy to obtain in that part of the world in 1862—and unrolled it, and a small doll appeared, a doll made of cloth, whose hair was of yarn raveled from the foot of an old brown stocking; whose eyes were black buttons, and whose scarlet mouth had been marked by beet juice. The doll wore a gay dress made of bits of yellow silk from Mrs. Arnold's scrap-bag. Her feet were covered with kid shoes, made from a worn-out glove, and the little hat, tied on with a bit of yellow silk, Berry had made by plaiting dried grasses.

"Mollie will like this doll, too," Berry thought happily, as she returned the package to its former place. "I wish there were some other little girls to ask to her birthday party," she thought, recalling her former playmates of the far-off Vermont village, where a birthday party had meant the gathering of at least a dozen little girls, all in pretty dresses, and each bringing a gift for the girl whose birthday they were celebrating. Berry smiled to herself as she glanced down at her stout leather boots and baggy knickerbockers. "They would all think my clothes as queer as Mr. Bragg does," she thought, recalling the full flounced skirts and embroidered pantalettes that she had worn before coming to Shiloh.

Snow continued to fall during the night, so that Mollie's feet were wet and her faded skirt more drabbled and limp than usual when she reached the Arnolds' cabin the next morning. An old brown shawl of Mrs. Bragg's covered her head and shoulders, and one end of it trailed behind her as she entered the pleasant kitchen.

Mrs. Arnold took off Mollie's shawl as she welcomed their little visitor, and Berry ran for a pair of moccasin slippers that Mr. Arnold had made from tanned sheepskin, and in a few moments Mollie's wet shoes had been set to dry and she was following Berry through the sitting-room to Berry's chamber, looking about as she always did with admiring eyes at the simple comforts of a home so different from the Braggs' dark, squalid cabin.

"Do you remember what day this is, Mollie?" Berry demanded as they entered her room.

Mollie nodded eagerly as she smiled radiantly up at her friend.

"'Deed I does. It's the day school begins!" she responded, her pale eyes shining with delight.

"And what else?" questioned Berry.

Mollie's smile faded and her face grew anxious.

"I dunno, Berry. It's snowing; you don't mean that, do you?" she questioned, and Berry gave a gay little laugh, and leaning toward her kissed Mollie's cheek, saying, "Happy birthday, Mollie Bragg. Here you are, eleven years old to-day! And you forgot all about it!"

Mollie looked at her friend with wide eyes. "I 'most always fergits it," she replied. "I guess nobody ever said 'Happy birthday' to me before."

"Well, I'll always say it to you after this, always!" Berry declared. "If I go back to Vermont and can't say it, I'll write it," she promised; and it was a promise she remembered and fulfilled after the two little girls were separated by the long distance between Vermont and Tennessee.

As Berry spoke she turned toward the chest of drawers and said:

"Birthdays mean presents, and here are your birthday presents from Mother and me," and Berry drew forth a little petticoat of soft gray flannel, one that she had formerly worn, and the blue serge blouse and skirt.

"Slip off your dress, Mollie, and we'll see if they fit," urged Berry, laying the garments on her bed, and before Mollie had recovered from her surprise she found herself dressed in the warm petticoat and the pretty serge dress, and Berry was tying one of her own scarlet neckties under the wide sailor collar of the blouse.

"There, Mollie! Look at yourself!" and Berry swung Mollie about in front of the small mirror, where the little girl gazed admiringly at her new appearance. Then, with a sober face, she began to untie the strip of scarlet silk and to unfasten the blouse.

"Don't take them off, Mollie!" exclaimed the astonished Berry. "You are to wear them, to-day anyway."

"Are they mine? Truly?" asked Mollie, as if unable to believe that she could really own such beautiful apparel.

"Of course they are yours. I helped to make them, but it was Mother who planned them," responded Berry.

"O-ooh!" exclaimed Mollie; but before she could say anything more a bell in the sitting-room tinkled sharply.

"School! Father is waiting!" Berry exclaimed laughingly, and putting her arm about the blue-clad little figure she drew Mollie toward the door.

CHAPTER IV
A CABIN PARTY

There was nothing in the Arnolds' sitting-room that January morning to remind Berry of a schoolroom unless it was the little brass bell that stood on the table beside which Mr. Arnold sat. Berry was so much in advance of Mollie in the usual school lessons that her father realized it would be difficult to teach the two little girls at the same time. The slate Berry had used in the village school in Vermont, and a box of slate pencils lay on the table, and a large atlas, opened at a good-sized map of the United States, was spread out beside it. While Mr. Arnold intended that Berry should have a proper knowledge of grammar and mathematics, he felt that she should understand something of the government under which she lived; and this morning he called the girls to look at the map of the United States, thinking it a good plan for both the girls to learn the names and location of the various states of the Union.

"Where's Shiloh?" questioned Mollie, gazing wonderingly at the brightly colored spaces on the map which Mr. Arnold pointed out as the different states of the Union.

"Poor little Shiloh isn't even a village, Mollie; it is only the name of a log church on a mountain ridge in Tennessee," he responded. But before the year 1862 ended Shiloh was known all through the country as the name of the place of one of the most terrific battles of the Civil War and had become an historic spot.

"Here is Tennessee," continued Mr. Arnold; "and this blue line is the Tennessee River. Along here," and with a pencil he pointed out the course of the broad stream, "it sweeps for many miles along the boundary line of Alabama, then turns northerly, in this great curve, and flows past Fort

Henry, and pours its waters into the Ohio River. Right here is Pittsburg Landing."

Both the little girls exclaimed at this familiar name; for Pittsburg Landing was not many miles distant, and was the point where the river steamers landed freight for Corinth, eighteen miles distant.

Before the morning lesson hours were over Mollie had learned that Washington was the capital of the United States, where laws for the government of the Union were made. That the terrible war between the Southern and Northern States, with Francis Arnold in the Northern army and Len Bragg with the Southern troops, meant that the South wished to "secede," to leave the Union, and form a new government. If the Northern armies won, the negroes would be freed, and the North and South remain a united nation. If the South conquered the North, slavery would continue, and there would be two separate governments.

"My Pa says the South will win," Mollie announced. "He says they beat the Yankees at Bull Run," she continued.

"Yes, the Southern troops are valiant fighters," Mr. Arnold agreed; for he never forgot that the Union had been formed by South and North alike, and he hoped earnestly for a peace that would again unite them in a firm and lasting friendship.

Then, while Berry was learning the rules of a lesson in algebra, Mollie happily began her first effort in writing. The slate and pencil seemed a wonderful thing to the little mountain girl, and she patiently endeavored to copy the lines and letters that Mr. Arnold traced for her.

The clock struck twelve, and Mr. Arnold again tinkled the small brass bell, and said smilingly, "Pupils are expected to be in the schoolroom at ten sharp to-morrow morning." As he finished speaking the door into the kitchen opened and Mrs. Arnold said:

"This is Mollie's birthday dinner party, so she must lead the way to the table."

"O-ooh!" Mollie whispered softly to herself, a little flush creeping over her thin face as Berry gave her a gentle push toward the kitchen, where the round table was spread for four, and where Mollie's chair held the newspaper bundle containing the doll.

Mollie Bragg always remembered her eleventh birthday; and she always treasured the cloth doll, the only one she ever owned, and which she at once named "Mrs. Arnold." There were broiled partridge for dinner, that Mr. Arnold had shot in the ravine two days before; and baked potatoes; there were spiced pears, that Mrs. Arnold had put up the previous autumn; and crisp hot rolls and steaming chocolate, a great luxury. And then a marvelous thing happened.

When Mollie believed that the dinner was quite over, and was again holding "Mrs. Arnold," and almost too happy to believe in so much good fortune, Mrs. Arnold went to the pantry and came back bringing a round white-frosted cake, on which stood eleven tiny pink lighted candles.

"O-o-ooh!" again murmured Mollie, as Mrs. Arnold set this wonderful creation in front of her little guest.

"Your birthday cake, Mollie! Wish! Wish for something splendid. Then try to blow all the candles out with one breath, like this," and Berry puffed out her cheeks and blew so strongly that the little flames wavered. "If all the candle flames go out your wish will come true before your next birthday," Berry concluded earnestly.

Mollie promptly obeyed Berry's directions, with such good success that every tiny flame was extinguished.

"Goody! Goody! But you mustn't tell your wish until next birthday," cautioned Berry, running around the table and carefully removing the candles from the cake. They were the same candles that had been used on Berry's own cake on her eleventh birthday in October, and they were now carefully put away. For who could tell when it would again be possible to purchase wax candles?

Then Mrs. Arnold helped Mollie cut the cake, and at the first taste Mollie smiled more radiantly than ever, but quickly put the piece back on her plate.

"Don't you like it, Mollie?" Berry asked anxiously.

"It's beautiful!" Mollie replied soberly; "but I'm goin' ter take it home ter Ma. May I?" she added, a little doubtfully.

"The whole cake is yours, Mollie dear. But you must eat the first piece yourself," Mrs. Arnold said quickly; "you are to take the remainder home."

Mollie drew a long breath. "I reckon my Ma never tasted a birthday cake," she said soberly.

After dinner was over and Mollie had seen Mrs. Arnold put the cake carefully into a small basket, which she told the little girl she was to carry home, Berry and Mollie went back to the sitting-room; and Berry brought out her own two fine dolls, which had heads of china with black curls painted on them, and were dressed in white muslin and wore sashes of blue silk. Berry had brought these dolls from Vermont, and one was named Josephine Maria, for Berry's Grandmother Arnold, who had given the dolls to Berry, and the other was called Maria Josephine. "Then, you see, neither one can be the favorite," Berry explained, as she set the dolls side by side in her father's big chair. "Now let's play it's a real party; my dolls and your doll can be 'real' girls, and we'll talk for them," she continued.

Mollie nodded with smiling delight, and for an hour or more the two little friends and their dolls played happily. But as the clock struck three Mollie announced that she must start for home.

"It gets shadowy and kinder fearsome in the woods come late afternoon," she said, "and my Pa says that niggers are runnin' off every little while, and maybe are hid up in the woods; so I'd be skeered to go home late."

"Don't be afraid of any poor colored man or woman who might be coming over the ridge, Mollie," said Mrs. Arnold gently.

"You mean niggers?" questioned the little girl; and then added quickly, "Oh, Mrs. Arnold! I never knew how grand it would be to be eleven years old, and have a birthday cake, and a doll, and a dress!" And she looked from one gift to another with so radiant a face that Mrs. Arnold felt well rewarded for her friendly efforts for her small neighbor's happiness. Berry had slipped on her cap and coat and was ready to go part of the way home with Mollie. Just as they had started Mollie suddenly turned back, and running to Mrs. Arnold she looked up at her and said earnestly, "I been tryin' to say 'thank you.' But 'tain't enough to say, fer all you give me. 'Tain't enuff jes' ter say, 'Thank you!'"

"Indeed it is enough, dear Mollie," responded Mrs. Arnold, leaning down to kiss the little face now flushed with the joy of her happy birthday.

Mrs. Arnold stood in the doorway of the cabin and watched the two little girls until the forest shut them from view. The snow had all vanished, the winter sun still shone warmly above the tree-tops, and only the caws of a passing flock of crows disturbed the perfect quiet of the scene.

CHAPTER V

LILY

Although Mrs. Arnold had told Mollie there was no need to fear the fugitive negroes who now and then made their way across the mountains, hoping to find freedom from slavery in the Northern States, the little girl's words made Mrs. Arnold thoughtful. Supposing a fleeing Tennessee slave appealed to her for a hiding-place, or for assistance to escape into Kentucky, which remained loyal to the Union, while Tennessee was a Confederate state, what could she do? Mr. and Mrs. Arnold both realized that, even on that remote mountain ridge, the fact that they were from the North, that their son was a soldier in the Northern army, would naturally prejudice Southerners against them, and if any member of the little household was discovered befriending a fleeing negro—who in those days was regarded as a piece of property by his master, and could be dragged back into slavery—it would place them in a dangerous position.

She spoke of it to her husband, but Mr. Arnold saw no cause for uneasiness.

"Of course, if any human being came to our door in need we would have to do what we could for him. Especially if it were a black man or woman; for they have never had a fair chance in this country, and we are bound to help them. I do not think there are half a dozen people beside the Braggs who know anything about us; and they are our friends," he concluded.

"Mr. Bragg declares he doesn't care which side wins," responded Mrs. Arnold. "He says he is 'neutral,' and that is why he is so angry at Len's running away to join the Confederate army. But I don't quite trust Steve Bragg."

While Mr. and Mrs. Arnold discussed the questions that were then causing so much trouble, Berry and Mollie had reached the brook and were saying good-bye.

Berry had carefully explained just how Mollie's doll had been made. "I spread out a piece of white cloth, doubled, and marked a doll out with a piece of charcoal, and then cut it out and stitched the two pieces together, just leaving a place open on top of the head, and then filled her with sawdust, sewed up the open place and covered her head with raveled yarn," said Berry.

"P'raps I can make one!" Mollie suggested hopefully.

"Of course you could," Berry agreed promptly.

"I'll make a black nigger doll, so's 'Mrs. Arnold' can have it for a slave," said Mollie.

"Oh! Mollie, you can't! That's what this war is about; to make white people stop making slaves of black people; it isn't fair!" declared Berry, and quickly added, "Mollie, why don't you give your doll an easier name?"

"I don't know any names. I loves your Ma, an' I loves this doll; so I calls the doll 'Mrs. Arnold,'" Mollie responded soberly, "an' I don' see no harm in makin' a nigger doll."

"Well, Mollie, my mother's name is Ellen; why don't you call the doll that?" Berry suggested.

"Oh! Yes! Ellen is lovely. 'Mrs. Arnold,' your name is 'Ellen,'" Mollie promptly informed her doll, holding it out at arm's length that she might better admire it.

"I'll start back now," said Berry. "School is going to be fine, isn't it, Mollie?"

Mollie vigorously nodded her shawl-covered head. "It's grand!" she declared; and then, coming very close to Berry, she whispered, "I've got a secret! Maybe I can tell it to you to-morrow!" and before Berry had time to question her, Mollie had taken the basket that held the precious birthday cake and started to cross the brook, making her way carefully from stone to stone. She did not leap from the broad stone to the opposite bank, as Berry delighted in doing, but followed the stepping-stones until the stream was safely crossed. Then she turned and called to Berry, who had stood waiting to be sure that Mollie crossed the stream in safety.

"I'm all right, Berry," she called. "I think it's fine to be eleven."

"What's the secret, Mollie?" Berry called back; but Mollie had turned and was hurrying off toward home. Berry looked after the little figure in the trailing shawl until it vanished in the forest path, and then turned and ran lightly up the ridge. A cold wind crept among the branches of the tall oaks as Berry ran; a rabbit leaped out from the underbrush and sped along before her for a short distance, and then vanished. Squirrels scolded noisily from the oak trees, and from the deep woods Berry could hear the distant call of some winter-loving bird. But the little girl hardly noticed these familiar sounds of the forest.

"I wonder what Mollie's secret can be?" she thought, and resolved to start out and meet Mollie the next morning. "Then she can tell me before lesson-time," she decided.

Berry had just reached this conclusion when her quick eye caught the movement of a dark object behind the underbrush that bordered the path. "A fox, maybe!" she thought, stopping to look more closely at the dark form. As she looked the figure raised itself from behind the underbrush and Berry gave a startled exclamation; for it was not a fox or any woodland animal that confronted her, but a young negro girl, evidently more frightened than Berry, and it was Berry who spoke first.

"What are you hiding there for?" Berry demanded. "Come out in the path where I can see you."

There were few negroes near Shiloh, and since coming to live in the mountain cabin the little Yankee girl had seldom encountered them. But she knew that Tennessee was a state where negroes were considered as the property of white masters; that negroes possessed no rights in regard to protection from cruelty and injustice. If they were fortunate in belonging to a kind master, and there were many such throughout the slaveholding states, they were well treated; but if owned by cruel, ignorant men, the negroes were abused; and it was from such unfair treatment that they frequently endeavored to escape by fleeing North. But, unless they could reach Canada, there was no safety for them in the Northern States, as the law of the Union, then, gave their masters the right to pursue them and force them to return. To end this injustice was one of the chief reasons for the Civil War.

As Berry looked at the frightened black face that peered at her above the underbrush she instantly realized that this was a runaway slave, and she again called:

"Come out in the path where I can see you," and now the negro girl crept out from her hiding-place and stood facing Berry.

"Oh, young Massa, don' mek me go back," she faltered. "I'se hongry an' col', an' I dunno 'zackly whar I be; but I reckons, if yo' jes' go on, young Massa, I kin git off so's I won't be kotched," and she fixed her big eyes pleadingly on Berry's face, her thin form, clad in a ragged garment made of coarse bagging material, shivering in the cold.

"I'm a girl," Berry announced. "You can't hide out in the woods; it's too cold. You'll freeze," she added quickly. "And you need not be afraid of me. I'll help you."

The negro girl stared at Berry as if even more frightened than before.

"Wot yo' dressed up dis way for?" she asked.

"Never mind about me," Berry replied, "but do as I say. If you will come with me you can have something warm to eat and drink, anyway. Then if you want to keep on running away you can."

For a moment the little white girl, rosy, well clad, and unafraid, and the gaunt, half-clothed, frightened black girl faced each other. Then a softer expression crept over the face of the negro girl, and she took a step toward Berry. "I'se gwine ter trus' yo', young Mass—Missie," she said softly.

Berry nodded. "Nobody shall hurt you," she promised soberly. "And let's run, or Father will be coming to find me."

But the negro girl shook her head dolefully. "I cyan't run, young Mass—Missie; my feetes is hurt," and now for the first time Berry noticed that the girl's legs were bare, and that her feet were protected from the rough, frozen ground only by worn pieces of cloth, tied about with string. And at this Berry exclaimed pityingly:

"Your poor feet! Well, we'll go easy," and she clasped the girl's thin arm, and started forward.

The negro girl did not speak again until they came in sight of the cabin, then she stopped suddenly. "Yo' ain' gwine ter let nobuddy sen' me back ter Alabamy?" she asked fearfully.

Berry's clasp on the girl's arm tightened. "I am going to help you, I am going to be your friend!" she promised earnestly. And the slave girl, meeting the pitying, friendly glance of Berry's brown eyes, was convinced that the impossible had happened; that a runaway slave girl had really found a friend. From that moment she had full confidence in Berry; whatever Berry told her to do she did instantly, sure that no harm could befall her as long as Berry was near.

"What is your name?" Berry asked, as they reached the porch.

"My name's Lily."

Berry pushed open the door into the kitchen, still clasping her companion's arm. "Mother, here is Lily!" she announced.

CHAPTER VI
SECRETS

Mrs. Arnold was busy at the kitchen table when Berry's announcement: "Here is Lily!" caused her to turn toward the door, and it was small wonder that for a moment she was too surprised at the sight that confronted her to speak. But she quickly realized what had happened, that Berry had encountered a fugitive slave girl and brought her to the cabin, and poor Lily's frightened, pleading eyes, as well as her half-clothed, trembling form, instantly appealed to Mrs. Arnold's sympathies.

"Come right to the fire, Lily," she said kindly. "And, Berry, you would better heat some milk at once."

Mrs. Arnold did not ask any questions. She could see that the negro girl was worn out by fatigue, hunger and cold, and promptly began to make her comfortable, bringing a warm blanket from the little chamber off the kitchen, where Francis had formerly slept, and wrapping it about the girl, who, silent, and still inclined to be afraid, sat stiffly on the wooden kitchen chair near the stove. Berry had instantly slipped off her cap, jacket and mittens, and put on a long gingham apron, that at once changed her appearance from that of a slender, alert boy to a curly-headed little girl. And as the shivering Lily watched her new friend set a small dipper filled with milk on the stove, and hurry back to the pantry for bread which she proceeded to toast and liberally spread with butter, Lily's face softened and she became sure that this wonderful little person, who had brought her to warmth and shelter and promised to protect her, was really a girl.

Lily ate ravenously. The hot milk and buttered toast disappeared so quickly that Berry hurried to the pantry for the remains of the partridge, left from dinner, and for more bread, and a new supply of milk, all of which the negro girl devoured.

"I ain't et rael food fer days," she whispered, looking up at Berry. "An' I neve' 'spected I'd hev a chanst ter eat agin."

While Berry was providing food for this unexpected visitor, Mrs. Arnold had filled a big kettle with water and set it on the stove to heat. The door into Francis's room was open, and Mrs. Arnold had placed a small tub there, and by the time Lily's appetite was satisfied the water was ready and the tub filled. Taking soap and towels Mrs. Arnold told the negro girl to follow her, and the surprised Lily was soon after introduced to the first hot bath of her life. Then, clad in a warm flannel wrapper, she curled up on the cot bed and was fast asleep when Mrs. Arnold returned to the kitchen.

Berry told her mother the story of finding the fugitive slave girl hiding on the side of the ridge, and Mrs. Arnold listened with a grave face. "It was so cold, Mother, and she was so shivery and frightened, I had to bring her home. And you said that of course we must help anyone who needed help," Berry pleaded, half afraid, by her mother's serious face, that she did not approve of Berry's having brought the negro girl home.

"Of course, Berry dear, you did exactly right. It has begun to snow again, and the poor creature would have perished if you had not brought her to shelter. She looks half-starved," and Mrs. Arnold wondered to herself at the courage of this young slave girl who had started out in midwinter, facing the dangers of the forest, of hunger and cold, and of probable pursuit, capture and punishment, rather than remain a slave.

"But you look as if you wished I hadn't, Mother!" said Berry.

"Do I?" and Mrs. Arnold smiled at Berry's troubled expression. "Well, my dear, I was wondering what we can do with Lily. You know slaveholders always try to find a runaway negro, and if Lily's owner comes after her and finds her here, he would have a right to take her. That is the law, and we could not prevent her going."

"It's a horrid law!" Berry declared, and her mother promptly agreed. "But, Mother, perhaps Lily's master may not even try to find her, and then Lily can stay here," the little girl continued hopefully, and Mrs. Arnold assented, saying:

"We will see what Father says when he comes in. Of course the girl must stay here for the present."

Mr. Arnold had gone to the little clearing further down the ridge where stood the rough log shelter that he had built for the cow, and when he entered the cabin Berry and her mother were eager to tell him of Berry's encounter with the negro girl, and that Berry had promised to befriend her, and had brought her home; and greatly to Berry's delight, and to the relief of Mrs. Arnold, he did not appear to be greatly troubled by Lily's presence in the cabin.

"We'll find out more about her, when the girl is well rested. Very likely her owner won't bother to look for her," he said; "but I don't know what we can do with her," he added.

"Oh, Father! There are lots of things Lily could do," Berry assured him eagerly, quite as if she had known the negro girl all her life, and Mr. and Mrs. Arnold smiled at their little daughter's evident adoption of the fleeing Lily.

The wind, thrashing among the branches of the forest trees, and the cold rain that had followed the fall of snow, made the blazing fire in the Arnolds' sitting-room seem even more pleasant than usual that evening, as Berry drew her small rocking-chair near the hearth. Berry's thoughts were occupied with Lily: she was sure that Lily must have had wonderful adventures, and looked forward to hearing them. She had entirely forgotten Mollie's "secret," and was earnestly planning how Lily could be provided with clothing. While Berry's thoughts were filled by this new adventure that had befallen her, Mr. and Mrs. Arnold were talking of the Union armies, and of the troops under General Ulysses S. Grant, a quiet, unostentatious officer, whose name was to be linked with the mightiest achievements of the Civil War.

"Grant's soldiers are now on their first campaign, untrained and unused to war. But most of them are from the West, hardy and brave, and if Grant moves against Forts Henry and Donelson it will open the Cumberland and Tennessee Rivers, and carry forward the Union front of war two hundred miles,—for General Grant would have Foote's fleet of iron-clads on the river to make victory sure," declared Mr. Arnold.

"If the Tennessee is once opened there will be conflicts near Pittsburg Landing, at Corinth—perhaps even nearer to us than that," responded Mrs. Arnold anxiously.

Mr. Arnold acknowledged that might be possible. "But, even so, we could not be in a safer place than in this mountain ravine. An army might march by on the Corinth road, or arrive at Pittsburg Landing, without troubling us. I am much more anxious about Berry's adventures with these wanderers along the trails than I am about armies and battles coming to Shiloh," he said, and at the sound of her own name Berry jumped up and ran to the big settle where her mother and father were sitting.

"What army, Father?" she asked.

"General Grant's army of West Tennessee, and the Confederate army of Commander-in-Chief Albert S. Johnston," replied her father. "Are you going to meet strange woodsmen or fleeing negroes every time you leave the house?" he added, smiling down at Berry's serious face.

"I wish spring would come! I'm tired of winter," said Berry.

"It won't be long now," her mother declared. "If the weather turns warm after this storm the catkins will begin to show on the alder bushes, the wild geese will come flying over, and spring will be close at hand. But it's bedtime, Berry, dear, so say good-night and be off."

"May I peek in and see if Lily is asleep?" asked Berry, and at her mother's smiling nod the little girl ran to open the door into the little room where the negro girl slept in safety.

The Arnolds had finished breakfast the next morning before there was any sound in the adjoining chamber. Mrs. Arnold had selected some part-worn garments for the negro girl, and in a little while Lily appeared in the kitchen, a very different Lily from the ragged, frightened Lily that Berry had brought home. She was eager to help in the work of the cabin, and before the hour for lessons arrived Mrs. Arnold realized that Lily had been well trained as a house servant.

"Do not ask Lily any questions, Berry," her mother cautioned. "Wait until she is ready to tell us her story," and Berry, a little reluctantly, agreed, for she was eager to hear of Lily's journey, and of her escape from slavery.

At ten o'clock the little bell tinkled warningly, and Berry hastened to the sitting-room.

"Mollie has not come," she announced.

"We will have to plan extra studies for pupils who are late or absent," said Mr. Arnold.

"Oh, Father! You said that just like a real teacher," said Berry. "Are we not going to wait for Mollie?"

"No, indeed! You and I will read a while," replied Mr. Arnold, opening a book on the table.

Berry looked at him questioningly. "But reading isn't lessons, Father! It's just fun," she said, a little note of reproach in her voice.

"Listen to this, and then, when I finish, repeat as much of it as you can remember," responded Mr. Arnold smilingly.

"'Pansies, lilies, kingcups, daisies,

Let them live upon their praises;

Long as there's a sun that sets,

Primroses will have their glory;

Long as there are violets,

They will have a place in story.

There's a flower that shall be mine,

'Tis the modest celandine.'"

"Father! That's not a lesson. I can say it all," declared Berry, and indeed she could, so well had her memory been trained in this very way, repeat Wordsworth's beautiful lines without a mistake. The lesson in algebra followed, and the morning hours of study ended without Mollie appearing.

"Probably she doesn't want to come," said Mr. Arnold.

But Berry and her mother were sure that was not the reason that kept Mollie away.

"May I go down and find out why she did not come?" asked Berry, as she sat down at the dinner table.

"No, I'm not willing for you to go down the trail to-day," said Mrs. Arnold quickly. "Perhaps Mollie will appear this afternoon."

"Perhaps she will," agreed Berry hopefully; "and I guess she will be surprised to see Lily," and she smiled at the silent Lily, who stood in one corner of the kitchen with her eyes fixed wonderingly upon her new friends.

CHAPTER VII
A SURPRISE

When the third day passed without Mollie appearing at the Arnolds' cabin Mrs. Arnold gave Berry permission to go and find out the reason. There were not to be any lessons that morning, as Mr. Arnold had not been well for several days, and it was Lily who cared for the cow, brought the milk to the cabin, the wood from the shed, and did all the chores that Berry's father usually did about the cabin.

"Isn't it lucky I found Lily?" Berry asked soberly, as she made ready for her tramp over the ridge to the Braggs' cabin.

"Lily is a great help," Mrs. Arnold replied, but she did not tell Berry that the fact of having the fugitive slave girl in the house might prove a great danger to the Yankee household on the Tennessee mountain ridge.

"Do not say a word about Lily to Mollie or to Mr. and Mrs. Bragg," Mrs. Arnold added, and Berry promised, thinking that whatever Mollie's secret was it could not be more wonderful than the discovery of Lily.

"It's like spring," thought Berry as she strode along the leaf-covered path. "I smell it in the air." For it was one of the days of late January when, among the ravines and valleys of the Tennessee mountains, spring seems close at hand. The sun shone warmly down, and wrens, nuthatches and cardinals flitted about the forest. "It won't be long before the sap begins to run and we can make maple-sugar," thought Berry. For there was a grove of sugar maples not two miles distant from the cabin, and Berry recalled the previous spring when she and her father had tapped the trees, boiled down the sap and made maple-sugar. "And that's what we'll do this year," she decided happily, as she left the path for a moment to watch a scurrying partridge as it fluttered over the rough ground.

Berry had not gone far from home, however, before she was sure that she was being followed; that someone, keeping well out of sight behind trees and underbrush, was not far behind her; and she wondered if it might not be the man who, only a week earlier, had spoken to her at the brook crossing, and mistaken her for a boy; and at this thought Berry's hand sought the silver whistle.

"But the whistle wouldn't help to-day; Father is too ill to come," she thought; "but it might frighten anyone who was hiding," she decided. But Berry did not use the whistle. She was a fleet runner, and off she went at her best pace, sure that she could outrun any would-be pursuer. Nevertheless, by the breaking of twigs and the crashing noises in the undergrowth, the little girl knew that her unseen pursuer still kept her in view; and not until she reached the highway, along which she must go for a short distance before reaching the rough lane leading to the Braggs' cabin, did she believe that she was at last out of reach of her pursuer.

"I'll ask Mr. Bragg to go home with me," Berry resolved as she hurried up the lane, for she recalled the stranger's threats if she told of having seen him, and did not wish to encounter him again.

As Berry came in sight of Mollie's home she noticed that there was no thread of smoke rising from the chimney of the cabin; it had a lonely and deserted look, but Berry did not stop to think of this. She was sure that in a moment the door would open wide, and Mollie, smiling with pleasure at the sight of her friend, would give her a warm welcome.

Berry rapped on the door, and then gave it a little push. But the door did not open, there was no response to her knock, and Berry now noticed that the cabin windows on each side of the door were evidently boarded up on the inside.

"They've gone away! And Mollie did not tell me!" she exclaimed aloud, with a sense of angry resentment against poor Mollie.

"That was her old secret! All the time I was making her doll, and her dress, and when she was pretending to want to come to school she knew she was going off," thought Berry, tears of angry resentment and disappointment coming to her eyes.

It was to be many weeks before Berry was to hear the true story of the Braggs' sudden disappearance, and learn that poor little Mollie had not been given time to tell her great secret, or to say good-bye to the friends who had given her such a happy birthday.

For a few moments Berry stood on the worn stone that formed the threshold to the dilapidated cabin, wondering where the Braggs had gone, and if they meant to return. The boarded windows made her feel sure that they had no intention of coming back, and, with a mournful sigh, Berry at last turned from the cabin and started on her tramp back through the forest.

Her thoughts were so filled by Mollie's disappearance that she had entirely forgotten the possibility of again encountering the man who had called her "Berry Nees," and not until she had left the main road and chanced to see a crouching figure lurking behind an old stump near the path did she realize that whoever it was that had followed her from home was still watching her every step.

Almost without thinking Berry drew the silver whistle from her pocket and its sharp call sounded clearly through the silence of the woodland path, and came echoing back as if repeated by a dozen whistles, and instantly the crouching figure sprang upright and leaped toward the little girl, exclaiming:

"Don', Missie! Fer de lawd sakes, don' blow no whissel!" and Berry found herself clasped tightly by the thin arms of Lily, who whispered fearfully:

"Yo' don' know w'at a whissel might fotch, Missie. 'Deed yo' don'!" and her big, frightened eyes stared at Berry as if they were both facing some great peril.

Berry pulled herself angrily away from the girl's clutching fingers.

"Was it you who followed me all the way from home?" she demanded.

"Yas, Missie," came the faltering response.

"And you were hiding behind that stump to follow me home, I suppose?" she continued.

"Yas, Missie," replied Lily in a whisper.

Berry was now feeling herself a much abused person. To have Mollie, her only friend and playmate, disappear without a word of explanation or good-bye had been a bitter experience; to have felt herself pursued all along the forest trail by a possible enemy, and now to discover that she had been needlessly afraid because of this stupid negro girl, made her angry and resentful. Berry did not stop to ask why Lily had followed her, or to remember that the girl was still afraid of every sound, and felt herself safe only when near to the little girl who had befriended her, and angry words rushed to her lips.

"Don't you dare follow me another step! I don't want to see you again, ever!" she declared, and without another glance at the cowering figure, Berry hurried on up the trail. She no longer noticed the calls of the forest birds, or the sunshine that sent flickering shadows across the woodland path. Mollie was gone, she was sure she would never see her again, and that stupid negro girl had made her run all that distance down the ridge as if pursued by a mountain lion, she thought resentfully.

"I wish Francis was home," she half sobbed, as she drew near the cabin. "Everything was all right when he was here. I hate war!" For Berry realized that it was the war that had taken her brother from home to unknown perils and to certain danger, and left her alone with her mother and father in the cabin, remote from friends.

She ran into the kitchen and, almost ready to cry, exclaimed:

"Mother! Mother! Mollie's gone! The Braggs are all gone, and the cabin fastened up! And Mollie never let us know!"

"Perhaps Mollie did not have a chance, my dear," said Mrs. Arnold quietly. "I am sure she would have told us if she could. But the Braggs are not the only ones who have disappeared. Lily has run away from us. She disappeared just after you left the cabin. I don't understand her going, for she seemed to think herself safe with us."

Berry stood silent for a moment, and then said slowly, "Lily will come back. Of course she will."

"I hope she will; she was a great help; if your father has to stay indoors for a time I do not know how we will manage without her help," rejoined Mrs. Arnold.

Berry stepped back to the porch and looked anxiously down the path, but there was no sign of Lily.

"Come in, dear; it is no use to look for her. Something must have frightened her, and so she has started off, or else she is dishonest and ungrateful," said Mrs. Arnold.

When Berry told her father of the disappearance of the entire Bragg family, he declared that he was not surprised.

"Very likely Steve Bragg has heard that Commodore Foote's gunboats are ready to come up the Tennessee, and that General Grant is preparing to advance upon the river forts, or that the Confederate forces may move toward Corinth. For Bragg is as much afraid of one army as of the other, and he has probably taken his family to some place farther from the river, and from the road to Corinth," he said, adding, "Poor little Mollie; her one day at school is likely to be her last."

"Perhaps they will come back?" Berry suggested, wishing she had not been so quick to blame Mollie for what it was plainly evident the little girl could not help.

"I do not think so," said Mr. Arnold; "but what do you suppose has become of your black Lily?" and her father's eyes rested questioningly on the sober face of his little daughter. Berry made no reply. She was beginning to be ashamed of her anger toward Lily, and to be sorry for her hasty words.

CHAPTER VIII
LILY'S STORY

Mr. Arnold had been right in thinking that Steve Bragg had removed to a location that he believed safer than the neighborhood of the Tennessee River in the late winter of 1862, and it was a long time before the Arnolds had any news of their former neighbors. But in her anxiety about Lily, Berry forgot, for the moment, that her playmate Mollie would not be on hand for their walks and games, and that henceforth she would be the only little girl on Shiloh Ridge.

Noonday passed, and the winter afternoon drew to a close, and Berry now became sure that they would never see Lily again. She thought of the friendless negro girl again wandering about without food or shelter, and trembling at every noise, and earnestly wished she had not driven her away.

Just at nightfall the outer door was cautiously pushed open, and Lily, her arms filled with wood, appeared on the threshold. Without a word, or a look toward the astonished Mrs. Arnold and the surprised Berry, she quietly filled the wood-box, and taking the milking-pail from its accustomed place started toward the door. Before she could reach it Berry called "Lily!" and started toward her.

"I knows yo' don' wan' me h'ar, Missie, an' soon's I do de chores fer yo' Ma I'll get my ole dress an' go," the girl said humbly, not raising her eyes to look at the little girl who had promised to be her friend, and who had then ordered her never to return to the cabin.

"Berry does not want you to go, Lily. Whatever made you think that?" questioned Mrs. Arnold. "We have all been troubled and anxious about you."

At the sound of Mrs. Arnold's friendly voice Lily looked up, and her eyes sought Berry's questioningly.

"Don't go away, Lily," exclaimed the little girl. "I don't want you to go."

A broad smile crept over Lily's face as she glanced from Berry to Mrs. Arnold. "Den I ain' ever gwine away," she declared, and started off with the milk pail toward the barn.

"Lily seemed to think you did not want her here. Poor girl. I wonder what will become of her," said Mrs. Arnold thoughtfully.

"Oh, Mother! You talk as if you did not mean for her to stay here!" Berry reproachfully responded. "And I told her to go and never come back!" she added quickly; and then Berry told the story of Lily following her to the highway.

"She kept out of sight all the way, Mother. But so near that I could hear her in the underbrush. And then, after I found the Braggs were gone, and started for home, and heard someone ready to follow me again, and found it was Lily,—and she acted so foolish and frightened, I told her I never wanted to see her again."

Mrs. Arnold busied herself with some work at the kitchen table, and for a moment made no response. It was Berry who was the first to speak.

"Of course I did not mean it, Mother. I want her to stay. I was only angry."

"I expect Lily is used to people being angry with her; perhaps that is why she ran away. It may be the reason that she would rather suffer cold and hunger, and flee in terror from every noise, rather than live with people who were easily angered," Mrs. Arnold responded quietly; "angry people are usually cruel people," she added, and before Berry could speak her mother continued: "The only reason that troubles me in regard to Lily staying with us is that your father and I might be accused of sheltering a runaway slave, and if she is found in our house it might involve us in serious trouble. You know, Berry, this is a slaveholding state."

"But no one knows she is here. And if anyone comes they will think Lily belongs to us," Berry responded eagerly. "And, Mother!" she added soberly, "I did not mean to be angry. I just couldn't help it."

Mrs. Arnold shook her head. "That's what everyone thinks, my dear. But even if you were angry it was no excuse. Lily followed you because she loved you: if any accident had befallen you on the way Lily would have been close at hand to help or protect you. I am sure that was her reason for following you. You see, Berry, you were the first one to help Lily, and she trusted you."

"Oh, dear!" sniffed Berry, ready to cry as she remembered that Lily had not tasted food since early morning, and had believed herself deserted by her new friend.

"And she came back to do your chores," she whimpered. "I'll make it up to her, so she will know I didn't mean it," the little girl declared, and when Lily brought in the milk it was Berry who ran to meet her and declared:

"Oh, Lily! We couldn't manage without you," smiling up at the wistful-eyed negro girl, who beamed with happiness at the unexpected kindness.

"I jes' follered yo', Missie, 'cos I was feared fer yo'," she whispered. "I didn' mean no harm!"

Berry nodded. She did not want Lily to see her cry, and so she ran off to the sitting-room to tell her father the good news of Lily's return.

As the days passed and no one appeared in pursuit of a runaway negro girl, the little household in the hillside cabin became sure that, at least for a time, Lily was safe, and Mrs. Arnold came to feel that Berry might be right in thinking that chance visitors to the cabin would believe Lily belonged there, and, as a week went by before Mr. Arnold could venture very far from the cabin, Lily became Berry's companion when the little girl journeyed down to the mail-box on the Corinth road, and in her walks along the mountain paths. And as the two girls wandered about together Lily told her new friend something of her pitiful story.

"I reckons I had a mammy sometime, but I don' 'member her. I was raised in Alabamy, Missie; an' ev'buddy wus allers a-givin' me a hit. Dey wus, show as yo' lib! 'Twan't de Massa and Missus, fer dey nebber seem ter see me; 'twere de niggers in de house dat batted me 'bout, an' I jes' made up ter run off. I hern de Yankee army wus a-comin' right soon ter set all de slaves free. Am dat a fac', Missie?" and the negro girl fixed her solemn eyes questioningly on the face of her little mistress.

Berry nodded. "My father says slavery must end," she declared solemnly.

"I'se glad! I hopes ebery one ob dem high-handed niggers dat batted me 'bout'll be set free an' hab ter look arter theirselves. Dat's wot I hopes. Wid no massa or missus ter feed an' tak' keer ob 'em!" said Lily, with a delighted chuckle, as if she felt that her wrongs would be punished by the freedom of her fellow-servants.

Berry looked at her in astonishment. "Didn't you run away to be free, Lily?" she asked.

"Yas, Missie, course I did. Dose niggers 'bused me. I had ter run off ter get clear ob 'em."

"Then you didn't run away from a cruel master and mistress?" continued Berry, wonderingly.

Lily shook her head. "I don' know much 'bout ole Massa; he go off las' year ter help Massa Jeff'son Davis win de war, and Missus she jes' went long wid him. I ain' nuffin 'gainst dem," Lily declared soberly. "'Twas dem stuck-up niggers dat batted me all de time, dat I runs off frum; an' I jes' hopes dey is gwine ter be set free," and Lily again chuckled, as if comforted by the possibility that her fellow-servants would soon be obliged to look after themselves.

As soon as they reached home Berry repeated the story of Lily's escape from the Alabama plantation. "She hid in swamps, and crept into barns to sleep, and ate corn, and frozen apples, and eggs. And it wasn't her master she ran away from!" said Berry, and then told her mother what Lily had said.

"Then we can feel safe about her not being followed, or a reward offered for news of her!" said Mrs. Arnold with evident relief. "Very likely her master does not even know that she has run away." And the little household was no longer troubled by anxious fears lest their kindness to the wandering slave girl might involve them in trouble, and Mrs. Arnold felt that Berry was much safer in her wanderings about the ravine with Lily for her companion.

And Berry soon discovered that the slave girl knew many interesting things about the little creatures of the forest. It was Lily who discovered the partridge eggs behind a fallen log not far from the cabin and cautioned Berry not to go near them or the partridge might desert the eggs. "Jes' keep 'way from dar, Missie, an' fus' t'ing dar'll be a flock of little partridges," she said. And it was Lily who heard the first call of the wild geese flying north, one morning in early February. It was Lily who tamed the two tiny woodland mice that peered out from under an old stump one sunny morning when Berry and Lily were resting near by. The negro girl cautioned Berry to be quiet, and attracted the tiny creatures with little calls until they stopped and fixed their bright eyes upon her, and even ventured near enough to eat bits of bread from the girls' luncheon. For several days Berry and Lily made daily trips to the old log with food for their new friends, whom they named "Dot" and "Dash," and the mice apparently were always on the watch for them.

When Mr. Arnold was again able to take his usual walks there were many hints of spring along the slopes of the ravine, and on one of his visits to the highway a traveler told him that the forts on the Cumberland and Tennessee Rivers had been captured on February 16 by General Grant, assisted by the fleet of gunboats commanded by Commodore Foote. Fort Donelson had been taken, and General Buell was preparing to advance against the Confederate army at Nashville.

This was a great success for Northern forces, and the Arnolds earnestly hoped might help to bring the war to an end. But Mr. Arnold realized that it must bring the troops of both the Confederate and the Union armies further south, and who could tell how near the little mountain cabin might stand to some future battlefield? But he did not mention this anxiety to Berry, but cautioned her not to go to the road leading to Corinth. And Berry was now counting the days when the sugar-maples could be tapped, and sugar-making begin, when another adventure befell her that might well have proven a dangerous one had it not been for Lily's courage and faithfulness.

CHAPTER IX
THE WITCH'S TREE

"Mother! Can't Lily wear those old clothes of Francis's?" Berry asked one March day, when Lily had returned from a scramble up the ridge, with the old dress of Mrs. Arnold's, that she had worn since coming to the cabin, so badly torn by the thorns and underbrush that it was no longer fit to wear.

"She can't climb trees, or run as fast as I do, or anything in that long skirt," complained Berry, and added quickly, "And she would like to wear things like mine."

"Yas'm!" Lily agreed hopefully, looking admiringly at her little mistress.

"Why did I not think of it before!" exclaimed Mrs. Arnold, who had been puzzled to know how to obtain clothing for the negro girl. With Northern armies advancing into Tennessee, and with General Johnston at the head of the Southern forces at Nashville, the family in the mountain cabin would have no opportunity to procure clothing. Mrs. Arnold realized that it might be months before it would be safe to venture to any of the neighboring towns, and that they must take every possible care of their supplies; therefore Berry's suggestion that Lily should wear the outgrown garments of Francis seemed to solve a difficult problem, and Mrs. Arnold, closely followed by Berry and Lily, hastened to open the old trunk in the small chamber where Lily slept, where Francis's part-worn clothing was packed.

"Here are some very good shoes," said Mrs. Arnold, as she took out a pair of stout leather shoes. "Try them on, Lily." The negro girl promptly obeyed, and they proved a fairly good fit.

Then Mrs. Arnold drew forth the brown corduroy knickerbockers, and the patched flannel blouse which her boy, who was now so far away with the Army of the Potomac in Virginia, had worn in the early days of their stay in the mountain cabin.

Lily was soon dressed in these comfortable garments, and Berry jumped about in delight as she exclaimed: "Now, Lily, we'll see who can run the faster, and if I win you can't say it is because you wear long skirts."

"Dat's de truf, Missie Berry. But I reckons yo'll win anyways," responded Lily, her solemn eyes fixed admiringly on Berry.

That afternoon Berry raked the leaves from her garden bed, and began to make plans for the border of wild flowers that she would transplant from the slopes of the ravine, or from sheltered places in the wood. On the previous day she and Lily had discovered the butterwort in bloom near the wide brook, where she had encountered the threatening stranger, its pale yellow flowers nodding from their slender stems above its flat rosette of curious leaves. It was one of the earliest blooms of the year in that part of Tennessee, and Berry was eager to bring home enough of the plants to brighten her garden border, as she knew the butterwort would continue to blossom through March; and early in the afternoon, with Lily as her companion, she started off toward the brook. Lily carried the large basket in which they planned to bring the plants home.

There were many hints that spring was close at hand. Robins and cardinals flitted about among the tree-tops, squirrels scolded and chattered, and little wood-mice now and then scampered out from shelter. As the girls came out from the forest Berry stopped suddenly and looked about in delight. "The red-bud is in blossom!" she exclaimed, for the tall, slender "Judas-Trees" growing along the borders of the forest, and standing in small clumps in the open clearing, had put forth their crimson buds and blossoms, brightening the leafless branches, and making the woods glow with color.

"I knows dat tree; it's de witch tree!" Lily declared solemnly. "Dat tree grow all 'bout in Alabamy. An' all de niggers uster tell dat, 'long 'bout midnight, witches comes ter dese trees an' meets up wid one anudder, an' makes der plans!" and Lily shook her head, as if feeling it was hardly safe to speak of such dangerous subjects.

"Do you really believe it is a witch's tree?" asked Berry.

"It shu' be, Missie. Dat's de reason it bust out, widout a leaf a-showin', in Feb'ry! Sum ob dose Alabamy niggers knows a sight ob t'ings 'bout witches. Ole mammy, what uster bang me right smart all de time I wus a-growin' up, she uster say dat if yo' could only be near one ob dese meetin's ob witches at dese trees yo'd h'ar strange t'ings!" replied Lily, rolling her eyes solemnly. "It's 'long 'bout dis time ob de year, w'en de blossoms show dat dey meets up an' makes der plans," she added.

"I wish I could see them," said Berry thoughtfully; "and, if they were good witches, perhaps they would tell me where Mollie Bragg is, and when she is coming home."

"Dar ain' no sich thing as a 'good' witch, Missie!" said Lily. "I reckons dey might tell yo' w'ot yo' wants ter know if yo' wus ter mak' 'em promises," she added thoughtfully.

Berry was now eager to know all that Lily could tell her, and, forgetting all about the butterwort, the two girls seated themselves on a moss-covered log near the "red-bud" trees, and Lily began the story she had so often heard on the Alabama plantation, of the proper way to secure the friendly assistance of a witch.

"'Course, Missie, yo' knows jes' w'ot a witch is. Dey's a kind ob black woman, wid wings. An' sometimes dey ain' no bigger dan a spider, an' ag'in, dey's big as a house! I knows all 'bout 'em!" declared Lily. "I wus bro't up 'mongst niggers w'ot had seen 'em! Yas, 'deed dey did!" and Lily nodded her woolly head so solemnly that Berry was convinced that her companion could tell her exactly the right manner to win the friendship of these powerful creatures who met at midnight beneath the blossoming Judas-tree.

"Yo' has ter take a sight ob trubble, Missie, ter meet up wid a witch, an' I dunno as I orter tell yo'," and Lily cast a troubled glance at her young mistress.

"Of course you must tell me, Lily!" Berry insisted eagerly. "Just telling me what people do to get a promise from a witch can't do me any harm. And sometime it might be a great help," she urged.

"Dat's so, Missie," Lily agreed thoughtfully, and, with a cautious look toward the flaming red-buds, as if even in daylight some careless witch might forget herself and appear at the chosen meeting-place of her kind, the negro girl drew a long breath and, leaning nearer to Berry, began, in almost a whisper, to tell the proper way to gain the favor of witches.

"Fus' t'ing ter do, Missie, is ter chuse de right time o' de moon. If dar be a moon showin' clar at midnight 'tain' no use! De berry bes' time am de dark ob de moon. An' yo' mus' be mighty near de tree, so's if de witches be de small kind yo' kin see 'em. But yo' mus'n' let 'em see yo'! 'Deed yo' mus'n', Missie!"

Berry nodded solemnly, and leaned a little nearer to her companion.

"An' yo' mus' fetch t'ings de witches likes. Dey is special fond ob fine honey," continued Lily. "Fac' is, dey likes sweet t'ings mighty well. Dat ole mammy I tells yo' 'bout, who banged me 'bout so, she uster mak' 'er fine cake long 'bout time de witch-tree blossom, an' put it near de trees com' dark, and dey witches allers kerry it off 'fore mornin'; dey shu did. I kinder 'magines dat ole mammy wus a relation to dem witches," said Lily thoughtfully.

"And what else, Lily? What else?" demanded Berry eagerly.

"Wal, Missie, I reckon dat am 'bout all: ter put de sweet t'ings near de tree, an' ter hide up clost so's dey won' see yo', an' den, w'en de hour of midnight come, an' dar ain' no moon ter be seen, and eberyt'ing am all black, den w'en de witches, each one ob dem carryin' a lille shinin' light on der heads, w'en dey begins to gather 'roun' de tree, den speak sof' an' remin's 'em ob de t'ings yo' set out fer 'em, an' ask 'em w'ot yo' wants ter know," replied Lily, adding quickly, "'Course dey mek yo' promise ter do w'otever dey wants yo' ter promise, an' I'se heard tell dat if yo' don' promise quick dey binds yo' up ter de tree an' leabs yo'."

Berry drew a long breath as Lily finished. The little girl was quite ready to believe that this negro girl really was sure in regard to the witches and their power.

"If I can find out about Mollie, and perhaps send her a message, it will be splendid," thought Berry; and then made the decision to try and win the favor of the witches who made the Judas-tree their meeting-place. But she said nothing to Lily of this resolve, and, as the negro girl took up the basket and they made their way to the borders of the stream where the butterwort was in blossom, neither of the girls even imagined that, close to the log where they sat, a man had been hiding behind the underbrush; a tall man, whose face was nearly covered by a brown beard; he wore a round, close-fitting cap of coonskin, a leather jacket, stout corduroy breeches, and high boots. A hunter's belt held a revolver and a hunting-knife, and if Berry could have had even a glimpse of this skulking figure she would have at once recognized him as the threatening stranger whom she had encountered near this very spot nearly two months earlier.

The man chuckled to himself as he watched the girls go down the little slope to the stream. "Berry has a nigger boy with him nowadays, eh!" he reflected. "That witch-story may be a help later on, for that white boy means to find out more about witches. Well, I'll send him over the road to Corinth at a good pace, or know why, when the time comes," he concluded, and slunk away in the forest. The man was a spy in the employ of the Confederate army, and was now traveling back along their line of defense, carrying messages from General Breckinridge, commander of the

Confederate reserves, who, only a little more than a year earlier, had been Vice-President of the United States, to General Beauregard, whose plan to concentrate the Confederate army of the Mississippi at Corinth was to bring about one of the greatest battles of the Civil War, the Battle of Shiloh.

The name of this man was Orson. He realized that the time was close at hand when a swift-footed messenger might be of the utmost importance, and in "Berry Nees," he believed he had discovered such a messenger. Orson was still sure Berry was a lad from some remote cabin, and meant very soon to make Berry prove the boast of being a fleet runner.

CHAPTER X

BERRY IN DANGER

Lily was interested in all the tiny wild creatures who lived along the mountain slopes, or made their homes near the creeks. She had queer names for many of these, calling the foxes "Sly-foot," and telling Berry many stories of the cleverness of Reynard. "Some darkies knows jes' how ter talk ter de wil' animiles. Dey shure does, Missie Berry. Dey knows w'ot ter say ter de fox. Dat same ole mammy w'ot tell me 'bout de witch tree she know how ter talk ter a fox or a sheep, or to de hawks dat hover 'roun'. She say to Sly-foot: 'Be yo' a good fox, or be yo' snoopin' 'roun' after chickens?' an' she know by de way de fox look dat he unnerstood. Mebbe de fox talk back, I dunno 'bout dat," Lily would conclude soberly; and as the two girls wandered about the mountain trails Lily's keen eyes were always searching path and thicket for a sight of some well-concealed nest or the hiding-place of tiny woodland creatures. Of each one of these she would have some story to tell, either of the way the birds built their nests, or of how weasels would spring from unseen coverts upon rabbits or squirrels.

Lily had made a rough bag of a piece of cloth that she had begged from Mrs. Arnold, and Berry noticed that the negro girl was always on the alert to discover and secure any feather that might drift across their path, or that had lodged on some wayside bush. Lily had fastened this bag to her belt, and not a day passed that some downy feather was not secured and safely put away. Sometimes she would be fortunate enough to discover a tiny red feather of the scarlet tanager, or perhaps a blue-edged quill from the blue jay, and on these fortunate occasions she would rejoice triumphantly. "Dat shure am fine!" she would exclaim with chuckles of delight.

"What do you want with all those feathers, Lily?" Berry would ask, but Lily would only nod and say:

"Jes' yo' wait, Missie Berry. Some day yo's gwine ter be s'prised!" and after a while Berry ceased to question her, believing that the gathering of these tiny feathers was only another of Lily's peculiar ways.

Beside securing birds' feathers Lily was always searching for the strong, pliant grasses that grew near the creeks. She would cut these grasses close to the ground with the greatest care, and tie them together. One day as the two girls climbed the slope toward Shiloh church Lily suddenly exclaimed:

"Dar! I b'en a-lookin' fer cedar, and har it be," and she left the trail and began to tug at the small trailing roots of a cedar tree. With the small knife that Lily always carried she cut and dug up portions of these roots, and then scraped off the soft bark, nodding and smiling her satisfaction. Berry's mind was entirely filled with possible plans for visiting the blossoming redbud trees at midnight, and with securing the necessary gifts by which the witches were to be made friendly and willing to answer her questions in regard to Mollie Bragg. A fine cake was not an easy thing to secure. The Arnolds' store of sugar was now very small, and Berry remembered that, in order to make the birthday cake for Mollie, her mother had said they must henceforth be careful in their use of sugar. Beside that, Berry could not offer a good reason in asking her mother to make a cake.

There was, however, no lack of honey in the mountain cabin, for, in the early autumn, Mr. Arnold had the good fortune to discover a "honey-tree," a partly hollow tree where wild bees had stored up honey, and Berry remembered with satisfaction that her mother had declared it to be of the finest quality. The little girl knew she could easily secure enough of this store of honey to satisfy any witch. But Lily had declared that witches were not easily influenced to friendly deeds, and Berry felt that the cake must in some way be obtained, and as soon as possible; for, with the approach of spring, Berry missed Mollie more and more, and was eager to try any plan by which she might get news of her absent playmate.

At the beginning of March, the week after Berry first heard of the possibility of securing the good-will of midnight witches, Mr. Arnold received news that General Buell, in command of Union forces in East Tennessee, had captured Nashville, the capital of Tennessee, and that General Johnston and the Confederate troops had moved southward to Murfreesboro. Thus, while the Confederates had won all the earlier battles of the conflict along the eastern line of defense, the capture of Fort Henry and Fort Donelson, and the taking of Nashville had restored the confidence of the North, and created vague terrors in the South.

Berry heard her father and mother discuss these happenings, and her father even declared that if General Johnston, with his army of 20,000 men, should join General Beauregard at Corinth, there would be 50,000 Confederate troops ready to meet General Grant's army if he moved against such a stronghold.

"Where would Grant's army come from?" Berry asked eagerly. "Would it march up the road from Pittsburg Landing? Oh! I could see it march from the big oak tree that hangs over the ravine!" she exclaimed eagerly.

"Very likely Grant's soldiers may be landed at Pittsburg and march over the ravine road," Mr. Arnold responded thoughtfully; "but, if they do, we may not know anything about it. Armies do not advertise the time of their arrival, my dear. And, for my part, I hope General Grant will choose another approach to Corinth. But you must promise me, Berry, not to go near the ravine road. Even now the Confederates may be on guard at Pittsburg Landing, and we must all do our best to keep near the cabin until we really know what Grant will do."

Berry promised, a little reluctantly. Pittsburg Landing was so far from the hillside cabin that Berry thought the road from there to Corinth, that led through a ravine not far distant, would be safe enough, even with soldiers at each end of it; and if armies, by any chance, should march that way Berry felt it a great pity to miss so wonderful a sight, for she was too young to realize all the terror and suffering brought by war, and she had not the faintest idea how soon she was to be almost in the centre of one of the most terrific battles of the Civil War up to the spring of 1862: the Battle of Shiloh.

When her father spoke of General Grant's probable advance against Johnston's army, Berry's thoughts were chiefly occupied with plans for a midnight visit to the Judas-tree, and she did not really believe it possible that troops might soon be on the march along those quiet roads near her home. It was now early March; Mrs. Arnold and Lily were busy with making a supply of soap: setting a barrel half-filled with ashes over which water was turned, and which was called the "leach-barrel," to drip into a big iron kettle; then the scraps of fat, that had been carefully saved for months, were boiled down over a fire in the yard, and strained; the lye from the wood-ashes was added, and again boiled, and a good supply of soft soap was the result.

These yard fires had to be carefully watched and tended; the soft soap, in its last process of boiling, had to be frequently stirred, and Berry and Lily spent the greater part of several days in the yard tending fires and kettles.

Beside soap-making there were other springtime affairs that required attention; it was time to tap the sugar-maples in the little grove on a distant hillside, and Mr. Arnold had begun to spade the plot used for a vegetable garden, so that every member of the little household was busy, and, until the day set for the visit to the maple grove, Berry and Lily did not go outside the fenced-in space about the cabin.

The day set for the visit to the maples was clear and sunny, and it was decided that the entire family should go, have a picnic dinner, and spend the greater part of the day on the hillside.

"We will find arbutus in bloom," said Mrs. Arnold, as they started out, Berry and Lily leading the way along the woodland paths. Berry had now discarded the long-legged leather boots that she had worn during the winter months, and wore moccasins, that Mr. Arnold had made for her, and as she went rapidly along the leaf-covered trail she made no more noise than a woodland squirrel.

Berry and her father tapped the maples: this was done by making a small incision into the trunk of the tree about two feet above the ground, inserting a tiny spout, and setting a pail under it to hold the sap; the next morning Mr. Arnold would come and gather the sap, turn it into a large kettle, and boil it down to a syrup.

While Berry and her father went from tree to tree, Mrs. Arnold and Lily searched the hillside for the arbutus blossoms, and carefully placed damp moss about the blooms they gathered to keep them fresh.

Mr. Arnold was busy with his work and did not notice when Berry wandered farther up the hillside, and when he had finished setting the pails, and the little girl was not to be seen, he supposed she was with her mother and Lily searching for arbutus, and looked about for a suitable place to start a fire over which to boil the coffee, and cook the bacon and potatoes for their out-of-door dinner. When this was well under way he opened the basket containing the food, and decided to surprise Mrs. Arnold by having the meal all ready before calling her, and it was nearly an hour later when his familiar whistle brought Mrs. Arnold, closely followed by Lily, scrambling up the hillside, each carrying a clumsily-made basket of twisted spruce and fir branches well filled with moss and the delicate, fragrant arbutus blossoms.

"It is like a May day!" Mrs. Arnold declared smilingly. "And how good that bacon smells! Frederic, I never was so hungry," and seating herself a short distance from the glowing bed of coals over which the bacon was cheerfully sizzling, Mrs. Arnold looked about for her little daughter, thinking Berry was close at hand.

Mr. Arnold refused any assistance, declaring no one could broil bacon over a wood fire as perfectly as he could do it; and not until Mrs. Arnold had been served with a well-roasted potato, bacon, and a plate of biscuit from the lunch basket set beside her, did Berry's father and mother look about for her, and then discovered that Lily had also disappeared.

"Berry can't be as hungry as I am or she would be on hand," said Mrs. Arnold, as the sound of Mr. Arnold's whistle echoed along the hillside.

"Hunting for flowers, but she'll soon be here, with Lily at her heels," responded Mr. Arnold, and added: "I wonder if we shall ever see little Mollie Bragg again?"

"I am sure we will," Mrs. Arnold replied. "Poor child, I am glad she was not taken away before we could give her a happy birthday to remember," and, talking of the Braggs, the time sped by, and yet no sign or sound of Berry or Lily. But neither Mr. nor Mrs. Arnold felt anxious as to the girls' safety. Berry had her whistle, which she would surely sound if in any danger, and, with Lily close at hand, it did not seem probable that any accident had befallen their little daughter, and only the fact that the potatoes and bacon would not keep hot at last decided Mr. Arnold to repeat his call, and finally to start back toward the maple grove in search of Berry, quite sure that he would find Lily with her.

Berry had not intended to go out of sight of her father when she wandered up the ridge, but the discovery of an unexpected trillium in blossom led her to go further on hoping to find more, and, by the time her father had started his fire, Berry was on the further slope, out of hearing of Mr. Arnold's shrill whistle. She had just decided to turn back when she noticed a tiny thread of smoke creeping up behind a ledge. Berry knew the dangers of a forest fire, and, thinking some careless woodsman had failed to put out his fire, she promptly started toward the smoke, meaning to put out the fire. Her moccasin-covered feet made no noise as Berry climbed over the ledge. As she looked down toward the thread of smoke Berry nearly lost her balance: for, just below, not twenty feet from the ledge of rocks where she crouched, was the threatening stranger whom she had met at the brook in January, and who had mistaken her for a boy. The man was crouched near a tiny fire over which he was roasting a partridge. If he had not been so intent upon his cooking he might have become conscious that someone was very close to him, for Orson was a thorough woodsman, with every sense on the alert. Berry, looking down upon him, realized that the man was camping there, as a rough shelter of boughs stood near by. She resolved to slip away as noiselessly as possible; with her eyes still fixed on the crouching figure, she cautiously moved one foot, and then the other, backward, holding to the rocks with both hands. There was a little noiseless movement along the ledge, and Berry felt both her feet held; a loose rock, started by her movements, had been gradually slipping, and now held Berry a prisoner. It had rolled against her ankles binding her to the side of the ledge.

"What can I do?" she wondered. To sound her whistle, even to endeavor to push the rock away, would instantly bring the man leaping up the ledge. "I must get clear myself, some way!" she resolved, but she could think of no way to free herself.

CHAPTER XI
THE MIDNIGHT ADVENTURE

Lily's wanderings during her flight from the Alabama plantation had made her alert and watchful of every woodland noise and sign. Since Berry had not come down the ridge with Mr. Arnold, Lily was sure she had followed a wandering path leading to the summit, and the negro girl sped swiftly along. At first she thought of calling her young mistress's name, but her instinct for silence prevented this, and, as she found herself facing the ledge where Berry was held prisoner by the rock that had slipped against her ankles, Lily had no impulse to cry out. As quietly as Berry herself she crept down close to the ledge, and noticing the thread of smoke a dreadful fear took possession of her.

"Lak as not it's fo'ks a-huntin' fer me. My lan'! W'ot I better do?" was her first thought; then her eyes turned toward the girl clinging to the ledge, the girl who had been the first to speak kindly to the fugitive slave girl, and instantly Lily recalled all Berry's kindness had meant to her, and she forgot her fears for her own safety, and thought only of her young mistress.

WITHOUT A WORD BERRY POINTED TO THE HEAVY ROCK.

"She be 'fraid ob dat man a-campin' down dar," she instantly decided, as peering from behind a sheltering tree she discovered Orson, still intent on his roasting bird. Lily crept up the ledge, whispering softly: "Missie Berry—Missie Berry," and Berry turned her head to find Lily's hand near her shoulder.

Without a word Berry pointed to the heavy rock resting against her ankles, and then toward the camp beneath the ledge, and shook her head solemnly, and Lily promptly understood that Berry feared to be discovered. Lily nodded her understanding of the message and cautiously worked her way to a place where she could make an effort to release Berry's feet. Pulling with all her strength she was able to raise the heavy stone so that Berry could draw herself free from its hold, and then, noiselessly as before, the negro girl lowered the stone gently back, and the two girls crept down the ledge and were soon safely in the shelter of the forest. Neither of them had spoken a single word since Lily's whisper when she reached the ledge.

But now Berry turned quickly to her companion and said gratefully: "Oh, Lily! What would I have done if you had not found me! And how clever you were to come so quietly! That's the man who threatened me near the brook, before you came," she added as they hurried up the rough slope.

"Dat man a-searchin' af'er me!" Lily declared solemnly. "Oh, Missie Berry, don' let him tek me! He's de kin' dat sells black fo'ks. I'se seen black fo'ks all chain' togedder, Missie Berry, a-standin' at railway stations to be tuk off." And Lily trembled at the thought of being discovered.

At that moment, before Berry could reply, Mr. Arnold's shrill whistle reached their ears and Berry instantly responded, and Lily had only time to say: "Don' say a wud 'bout dat man; don', Missie Berry! Promise!" she pleaded so urgently that Berry agreed.

"But I know he isn't after you, Lily," she added, as they ran forward to meet Mr. Arnold.

"Oh, Father! I got my feet caught in a ledge, and Lily helped me out," she explained hurriedly; "and we're both hungry."

Mrs. Arnold had contrived to keep the potatoes hot, and the two girls made an excellent lunch, while Berry told of finding the trillium blossom, and of climbing a ledge, and a rock rolling against her ankles.

"Lily came just in time, and moved the rock so gently that my ankles don't hurt a bit," said Berry; while Lily listened, fearful that some careless word might betray the secret. But Mrs. Arnold hurried them all toward home, as the March day was drawing toward sunset, and on the way Berry found a chance to tell Lily that the man they had seen was probably a Confederate spy. "My father says that General Beauregard has a Confederate army at Corinth, and probably this man is watching to see if General Grant's soldiers are coming this way," she explained to the frightened negro girl, and her explanation was the right one. Orson knew that numbers of Confederate soldiers were daily arriving from Mississippi, Louisiana and Alabama, in regiments, squads, or unarmed and singly at Corinth. All these were being formed into the Confederate army of the Mississippi, with General Johnston in supreme command, and with the brave and accomplished Beauregard as second. Supplies for this army reached Corinth over all railroads. Spies were bringing daily reports of the progress of Grant's army, and of General Buell's rapid approach from Columbia; and Orson was lurking along the roads from Pittsburg Landing to Corinth, ready to carry, or send, instant news of any approach of the enemy over these roads.

But Lily shook her head over Berry's explanation.

"He luk jes' lak de men dat hunt af'er de run'way niggers!" she insisted, and so Berry again agreed not to tell her father of her discovery of the camping spy.

Orson knew of the Arnolds' cabin, but kept a good distance from it, although he believed it the cabin of some industrious mountaineer who was, without doubt, loyal to the Confederacy. He had seen Lily and Berry more than once, unseen by them, and supposed Lily to be a negro boy, owned by the Arnolds. He meant, at the right moment, to send "Berry Nees" speeding over the road to Corinth with news for General Beauregard. He kept a nightly watch by the "witch-tree" to see if Berry had brought the sweets that would mean a midnight visit, and, on the second evening after the

Arnolds' visit to the maple grove, his watch was rewarded: for close against the trees rested a number of small packages.

Orson had no scruples in examining these. One contained a glass tumbler filled with honey, over which the spy chuckled, thinking it would be an acceptable addition to his somewhat limited food supply. In another package was a square of maple-sugar, made from the fresh syrup. There was also a small square cake, sweetened with maple-sugar, that Berry had persuaded her mother to make for her that morning. For Berry had noticed that the red-buds were beginning to fade, the leaves rapidly covering such blossoms as remained, and, by cautiously questioning Lily, she discovered that unless the tree were in bloom the witches were not apt to visit them, and she realized she must lose no time in asking their help for news of Mollie.

Berry found no trouble in carrying her gifts to the red-buds near the stream, for that afternoon Lily had gone with Mrs. Arnold to bring home the syrup that Mr. Arnold had made, leaving Berry alone in the cabin. And she collected her supplies and hastened off to leave them at the red-buds, in order that the witches might not fail to find them on their arrival, and she was resolved to be on hand when the witches appeared at midnight, although she was a little fearful that it might not be an easy matter to keep awake until the time came to leave the cabin, or to creep out without being discovered by her mother or father. Nevertheless she was resolved to make the attempt, for it seemed to Berry as if she could get news from Mollie in no other way than through the friendly help of witches, who were new possibilities in Berry's experience.

The sky clouded over before Mrs. Arnold and Lily returned, and by sunset a strong wind was sweeping along the ridge.

"Dis am a reg'lar witch's night! I 'clar ter goodness if 'tain't!" said Lily, as Berry helped her wash the supper dishes. "De win' am a-shreekin' an' ahollerin' jes' de way witches lik's," continued Lily; "dey'll all be out ter-night, I specs," and she rolled her eyes solemnly and shook her head.

Berry made no response. She heard the wind moaning and shrieking, as the big branches of the forest trees bent before it, and began to dread the undertaking that was before her. She was so quiet in the early evening that her mother was sure Berry must be more tired than usual, and suggested that the little girl go to bed. Lily had already gone to her room, and Mrs. Arnold declared that she herself was too sleepy to sit up, and at an unusually early hour the lights in the little cabin were extinguished, and the entire household, excepting Berry, were fast asleep.

In her own room, still fully dressed, Berry sat on the edge of her bed waiting for the clock to strike eleven, the time she had set to leave the cabin. More than once she dozed off, to wake with a sudden start fearful lest she had overslept. But when the clock in the sitting-room sounded the hour of eleven Berry was wide awake. Her window, that opened outward on hinges, was already partly open, and Berry's moccasin-covered feet made no noise as she crossed the room, cautiously swung the latticed window wide open and fastened it back, and then, reaching out, grasped the strong branch of the big oak tree, that grew close to the cabin, and fearlessly swung herself clear of the window-sill.

Berry had done this many times; it was no new exploit for the little girl to scramble along the stout branch and down the trunk of the oak tree to a secure footing on the slope of the ravine below her window; she stood silent a moment, looking up at the cabin. Then, sure that no one had heard her quiet escape, she crept up to the trail and was off toward the witches' tree.

The wind swept against her, and the trees of the forest creaked and swayed: the night was too dark even for shadows, and Berry, with a little thrill of fear, recalled Lily's words that it "was a reg'lar witch's night."

As she neared the brook she saw a tiny light near the place where she had left her gifts, and stopped suddenly; then, remembering that Lily had said witches usually carried tiny lanterns, she drew a long breath, and stepped boldly forward, bowing very low, according to Lily's directions, and putting both hands over her eyes: for Lily had said it would be a fatal thing to let your eyes rest upon a witch.

CHAPTER XII
ORSON'S MISTAKE

With bent head and covered eyes Berry stumbled toward the trees, and at the sound of her approach Orson promptly extinguished his pipe; the tiny light, that Berry had mistaken for a witch lantern, having been the match he had used in lighting it.

The little girl had just reached the clump of trees when, close at hand, a high-pitched voice called: "Halt! What seek ye at the witch-tree?"

Orson was so close to Berry that he could have touched her, and Berry gave a little gasp of terror at the sound of a voice coming, apparently, from the tree itself. But her question was ready, and, although her voice faltered a little, Orson could hear distinctly.

"If you please, kind witch, I want to know where Mollie Bragg is, and when I will see her?" said Berry.

"Do you intend to obey, and promise what I require, if I answer?" growled the voice, so near to Berry that she gave a little backward start.

To obey a witch seemed rather a dreadful undertaking, but Berry did not hesitate. "I do!" she faltered.

"'Tis well! You promise to come to this tree each day: to look under a flat rock at its roots, and when you find a letter there to take it and run your swiftest until you give it to the person whose name is written upon it?" growled the voice.

"I promise," said Berry.

It seemed to the little girl that the witch chuckled, and then there was a moment's silence. The wind died away, the thrashing branches of the forest trees gradually lessened, stars shone out from among the drifting clouds, and the darkness of the night grew less dense. Berry heard the movement of some large body close beside her, and knew that the witch would soon vanish.

"But tell me of Mollie?" she called anxiously.

"Boy! Mollie will soon return; watch for letters," came the response from some little distance. And now Berry uncovered her eyes and lifted her bowed head.

"Boy!'" she repeated in amazement. "Witches don't know everything after all!" she decided, "and it was so dark how could it see I didn't wear a dress?" And Berry was conscious of a vague disappointment, as she turned back toward the cabin. But the "witch" had said Mollie would soon return; and Berry told herself that this news was worth all her trouble. Then she recalled her promise, and wondered about the letter. To carry a witch's letter would, she thought, be something that had never before happened to a little girl. She wished she could tell her mother of this wonderful encounter with a witch; but Lily had said that one must never tell of such things or the witches would be angry. So Berry made her way back through the shadowy forest, climbed into her chamber-window, and crept noiselessly into bed. But she lay long awake thinking over her wonderful adventure at the witch's tree.

Orson was well pleased at his success in securing "Berry Nees's" promise to watch for any message the "witch" might leave at the Judas-tree. He lurked behind a stout oak until the little girl had made her way up the trail, and then started back toward his camp. If this "boy" could run as fast as Berry had boasted he knew it might prove the means of defeating General Grant when that officer should decide to attack the Confederates, and assured himself that he had been very clever indeed in making Berry believe that she had really encountered a witch.

Orson knew that Grant was determined to push on to the Memphis and Charleston railroad, and that Beauregard hoped to surprise and capture the Union Army of the Cumberland. To send the Confederate General news of Grant's approach would be a great triumph for this spy, and might, as he well realized, bring him a reward in the approval of Jefferson Davis, the head of the Southern Confederacy. It was therefore natural that he should think himself very clever in securing Berry's promise to become his messenger. Ever since he had overheard Lily's story of the witch-tree he had lurked about the place, confident that "Berry Nees" intended to ask a favor of the witches; and, on discovering the honey and cake he had promptly established himself close to the tree, thinking if Berry braved the darkness and the high wind it would be a good proof of "the boy's" courage; and Orson was well pleased to find Berry so fearless. "Plucky little chap," he thought approvingly, and almost regretted that he had not openly told Berry the service he meant to ask. But, on the whole, he decided he had chosen the better way. He was glad that he could now start off toward the Tennessee River, where he could keep a sharp outlook for any advance of the Union army.

Berry had not the slightest idea as she sped along through the darkness that close behind her came Lily; or that, when the voice had called, "Halt!" Lily, trembling with terror, had nevertheless moved a step nearer to her little mistress, ready, if need be, to risk any danger to herself in defense of Berry. She had been so frightened at Berry's question that it was a wonder she had not screamed aloud; but when Orson responded, calling Berry "Boy," Lily regained her courage.

"Dat ain' no witch!" she promptly decided; for the negroes of the Southern plantations firmly believed in the existence of unseen creatures, which they called witches, that knew far more than mortals; and Lily was sure that a true witch could not be deceived, and instantly she remembered the man Berry had met at the brook and whom they had seen at his forest camp.

"I reckon dat man am a makin' believe jes' ter skeer my Missie, or else he be up to somethin'," decided Lily; and, as Berry turned toward home, Lily moved quickly after the shadowy figure that was rapidly making its way from tree to tree.

It did not take Lily long to discover that she was right in her suspicion, and to recognize the tall, shadowy figure as that of the woodsman whom she had seen roasting a partridge near the ledge where she had discovered Berry.

"De misserbul critter," Lily muttered angrily to herself; "an' who know w'ot place he wan' my missie ter kerry a letter to? I jes' kal'ate I'll get dat air letter," and Lily now hastened after Berry, reaching the cabin just in time to see her young mistress clamber into the open window.

With a sigh of relief Lily crept silently to her own room. Although she had gone to sleep very early that evening she had awakened an hour before Berry left the cabin, and, prompted by a vague fear in regard to the safety of her young mistress, Lily had cautiously made her way through the shadowy rooms to the door of Berry's chamber and curled herself up there. Her quick ear had instantly followed Berry's movement toward the window, and she had been close behind the adventurous little girl as Berry scrambled down the trunk of the oak tree.

Both the girls slept late the next morning, and Mrs. Arnold watched Berry a little anxiously, for the little girl seemed unusually serious. "I believe Berry misses Mollie Bragg more than we have realized," she said to Mr. Arnold, after Berry had gone out to work in her garden, where the iris was already several inches high and where the transplanted butterwort was in blossom.

"I should not be surprised if the Braggs return to their cabin," Mr. Arnold replied; "Bragg is such a coward that the sight of the marching troops, of either the Confederate or Union army, will start him off; and he will not be welcomed by any community where brave men are willing to fight for what they believe to be right."

It was very hard for Mr. Arnold to feel that he could not serve his country. He realized now that from this remote cabin, perched on the side of a ridge of the mountains of Tennessee, he might watch the advance of General Grant's army of the Cumberland moving toward Corinth to attack the forces of General Johnston. Not for a moment did Mr. Arnold imagine that the task of the Union army would be one of defense, or that on the heights of Shiloh the Confederates would surprise and very nearly overcome the Army of the Cumberland; nor could it possibly occur to him that his small daughter was to render a great service to the Union cause, and to be long remembered as "The Yankee Girl of Shiloh."

Berry, busy in her garden, thought over her adventure of the previous night and wondered if the "witch" was right in saying that Mollie would soon return. "Father thinks they will come back," she reminded herself; for Berry could not forget that the witch had failed to discover that it was a little girl who had asked assistance. Nevertheless, Berry was resolved that not a day should pass without her visiting the clump of red-buds near the stream, that she might keep her promise to the witch and deliver any letter she might find there. And, quite unknown to her young mistress, Lily had resolved to be the first to discover any letter hidden at the witch's tree.

"An' I'll tek dat letter right ter Massa Arnold. Dat's w'ot I'll do. Mebbe 'tis 'bout me," Lily decided firmly.

CHAPTER XIII
BERRY RECEIVES A MESSAGE

Lily's "feather-bag," as Berry called the receptacle in which the negro girl so carefully stored each feather that she could secure, was missing from her belt one morning, and Berry at once announced the fact.

"Your feather-bag, Lily! Have you forgotten it?" she asked, as Lily appeared at the corner of the cabin and stood watching Berry who was busily engaged in transplanting woodland violets to the shady corner of her garden.

"No, Missie Berry. I knows jes' whar dat bag is. Yas'm, I'se got it hid up safe," Lily responded with her usual nods and chuckles. "I'se got all de feathers I wants," she added.

"Well, you must have nearly enough to stuff a pillow," Berry declared, wishing that Lily would tell her what she intended to do with the treasured feathers, but Lily only repeated:

"Yas'm," and Berry went on with her work. Lily immediately vanished, and did not again appear until it was time for her to help with the midday meal.

"I do wonder where Lily goes, and what she is up to," Berry confided to her mother. "Every day she suddenly disappears and is gone for an hour or two. She always comes back looking as well pleased with herself as if she had just discovered a pot of gold."

"Why do you not ask her where she goes?" questioned Mrs. Arnold. "Very likely she only goes off by herself for a nap, for she is up very early each morning."

"I have asked her," Berry responded, "and she just chuckles and nods and says that she hasn't been anywhere. 'Jes' kinder perspectin' 'roun''; that's what she says, Mother." And Mrs. Arnold smiled at Berry's imitation of Lily's voice and manner. But it was only a few days after this when Berry, coming into the sitting-room, discovered Lily peeping out from Berry's chamber.

"Lily! What are you doing in my room?" she called sharply, and the surprised Lily gazed at her a little fearfully.

"I jes' stepped in to take yo' somefin'. Somefin' ter s'prise yo'," she finally found courage to say, for Berry did not usually speak in so sharp a tone, and Lily was sure that she herself was to blame. "I wasn't lookin' fer yo', Missie," she went on, as if to excuse herself for some fault, but Berry pushed past the negro girl and entered her chamber. Her quick glance went straight to the dainty dressing-table and with an admiring exclamation she ran across the room and stood looking eagerly at the prettiest basket she had ever seen. It was shaped like a shallow bowl, and at the first glance Berry thought it was made entirely of feathers, but the feathers were only skilfully woven in broad bands through the sweet-grass that formed the warp of the basket. The woof was of the fragrant cedar roots; these Lily had split and polished until they shone like silver bands.

It was indeed a beautiful piece of work, and Lily's "surprise" was a great success. The negro girl had never before been so praised and thanked, and when Mr. and Mrs. Arnold were called to come and admire "Lily's basket," and when they also said that it was the finest basket they had ever seen, Lily was as happy as it was possible for a girl to be.

"Who taught you, Lily?" questioned Mrs. Arnold, and Lily told of the old negroes at the plantation from which she had fled, who were expert basket makers.

"I hears tell dey learned ter make baskets 'fore dey was fetch to dis country," she said, and Mr. Arnold remembered having seen feather baskets that were brought from Africa.

"And that's what you wanted feathers for; and that's what you have been doing when I wondered where you were!" Berry exclaimed, and she was now eager to learn how to make just such a basket, and Lily promised to at once begin gathering more feathers.

The basket henceforth was one of Berry's chief treasures, and years afterward, in her New England home, she would often show it and tell of Lily's "feather-bag."

As the days went on Berry was constantly discovering how many things Lily knew.

"Not the same things I know," she explained to her mother, "but wonderful things. Lily can make all sorts of things out of tiny twigs; she can make dolls and birds; long-legged cranes, that look just like those that Father and I have seen along the river." And Lily could indeed twist the pliant willow twigs into many shapes, over which Berry would laugh delightedly.

The spring days went rapidly by, and it was now months since the Arnolds had received any word from their soldier son, Francis, and visits to the post-box on the Corinth road only brought disappointment. One morning, toward the end of March, after her unfailing daily visit to the clump of Judas-trees, Berry decided to visit the box and then to go on to the Braggs' cabin and see if there was any sign of the witch's promise of Mollie's speedy return coming true.

Much to Berry's surprise there was something in the box. But she quickly discovered that it was not the hoped-for letter, for her hand had closed on a smooth roll of birch-bark. Berry drew it out and looked at it wonderingly. There were a number of queerly-shaped letters traced on its smooth surface.

"I wonder who put this in our box?" she said aloud, and then suddenly she waved the bark triumphantly and exclaimed, "Mollie! Mollie did it. She makes letters just that way. This means Mollie's home!" and Berry started off toward the wood road leading to the Braggs' cabin, sure that Mollie would come running to welcome her, and thinking happily of all she would have to tell and of all Mollie's probable adventures of which she would hear. She looked eagerly for some trace of smoke rising from the cabin chimney, but there was none to be seen, and as she came to the rough clearing about the cabin Berry stopped suddenly.

"They're not there!" she exclaimed; for the windows were still boarded over and there was no sign that the dilapidated cabin was again inhabited. Berry, standing near a sheltering clump of fir trees, felt almost ready to cry over her disappointment. She still held the roll of bark in her hand, and now again looked at it. The letters M. and B. were clumsily traced with a bit of charcoal on the smooth surface of the bark, and were followed by the lines and curves such as Mollie had drawn on the slate during the lesson hour in the Arnolds' sitting-room. "I am sure Mollie wrote these," Berry whispered, "and that she put them in our box as a message to me. She must have been here;" and Berry's eyes again turned anxiously toward the cabin, but there was nothing to be seen to indicate that the Braggs had returned.

Berry decided that she would go home by a woodland trail that led from the back of the cabin through a thick growth of forest trees toward the stream which ran down from the Shiloh plateau, and she walked slowly across the clearing and to the back of the cabin. Her moccasin-covered feet made no noise, and as she turned the corner of the cabin she heard the familiar voice of Mrs. Bragg and saw that the back door was ajar. Berry's first impulse was to run toward the open door, but at that moment she heard Mrs. Bragg say, "No, Mollie! How many times must I tell ye that yer can't see Berry Arnold? Didn' yer Pa warn us ter keep ter ourselves till he lets us know which army's gwine ter win? I reckon we kin stan' bein' a little hungry, an' I reckon Berry's fergot ye 'fore this!"

"Oh! Mrs. Bragg! I haven't!" Berry exclaimed, darting forward and pushing open the cabin door. "Why don't you want us to know you are home? Oh, Mollie! I'm so glad to see you!" and Berry ran toward the thin little figure that, at the sound of her voice, had jumped up from the wooden stool in a far corner of the room.

"Oh! Berry! Berry!" sobbed Mollie, as she felt Berry's firm arms holding her tightly; and for a moment the two little friends quite forgot Mrs. Bragg and everything except the joy of seeing each other again. It was Mollie who spoke first. "My nice dress is spoiled," she said, and Berry's swift glance noticed that the serge skirt had evidently been torn and clumsily mended, and the blouse showed that it had received hard wear. The kitchen was cold and dark, and Mrs. Bragg explained that Mr. Bragg had warned her not to start a fire for fear some wandering spy might discover that the cabin was inhabited.

"Steve says Corinth is chuck full of Confederate soldiers and that the Yankee soldiers have landed at Crump's Landing, not more'n ten miles from here; the Yanks tore up a good stretch of railroad between Corinth an' Columbus, an' Steve says thar's more Yanks on the march from Columbia; an' Steve jes' put off ter the mountains. He'll cum back soon's these pesky armies goes off," Mrs. Bragg explained, as if thinking it only natural that Steve should flee from any possible danger.

"But we have fires, Mrs. Bragg; and no American soldier, Confederate or Yankee, would harm you," Berry declared. "Why, Mrs. Bragg, perhaps your own boy, Len, might get a chance to come and see you if the Confederates come this way; and if the cabin is all shut up he would think you had all gone away, and he would go off and you wouldn't see him," said Berry eagerly.

For a moment Mrs. Bragg stared at her little visitor in amazement; then, moving toward the fireplace, she exclaimed, "My lan'! That be the very truth. Yo' gals fetch me some kindlin'-wood an' I'll start up a blaze. An' I'll wrench them boards off'n the windows and open the front door——"

But a shrill scream from Mollie brought her mother's plans to a sudden end. Looking toward the open door Mollie had discovered a stranger; a young negro boy stood there peering anxiously into the cabin; for Lily never permitted Berry to be long out of her sight and had followed her to the post-box and then on to the Braggs' cabin.

"It's only Lily!" Berry explained. "She is living with us, and wearing Francis's old clothes because they are easier to go about the woods in."

"Dat's so!" agreed Lily solemnly, looking first at Mollie and then at Mrs. Bragg.

"I declar'!" exclaimed Mrs. Bragg. "Wal, then she can take hold and holp us git this cabin fit ter live in. Ter think I didn't project Len comin' this way!" and Mrs. Bragg was now as eager to get a fire started, to open the windows, and give the cabin the look of being in use as, a few hours earlier, she had been to hide away from any possible visitor.

"It's a blessin' you happened this way, Berry!" she declared. "Yo' jes' tuck that roll of nice birch-bark under those sticks," she added, noticing the roll of bark, on which Mollie's message was traced, that Berry still held.

With a smiling glance at Mollie, Berry promptly obeyed, and in a moment the bark blazed up, the kindlings caught fire, and a cheerful glow and warmth filled the room. With the help of Berry and Lily the boards were taken from the cabin windows and Mrs. Bragg did her best to put the poor rooms in order. When Berry declared it was time for her to start for home Mrs. Bragg cheerfully consented for Mollie to go with her, and with Lily close behind them, the two little friends made their way along the forest trail.

Berry listened eagerly to Mollie's story of the wandering life the Braggs had led since leaving their cabin.

"We visited Paw's cousin first," Mollie explained, "but he wanted Paw to jine up with the Tennessee sojers an' go ter Corinth, but Paw don' b'lieve in fightin', so we went on. We lived in a cave fer a spell. An', Berry, mos' days I've bin hungry!" concluded the poor little mountain girl, looking up at her friend as if appealing for protection.

"Well! you shan't be hungry again, Mollie!" Berry promised. "And we have lots of new maple syrup; and I'll ask Mother to make batter-cakes for our dinner to-day!"

Mollie's pale eyes brightened at this unexpected delight. She was sure her troubles were over now that Berry was with her.

"I hoped you could read what I wrote on the birch-bark," she said, as they came in sight of the Arnolds' cabin. "I put it in the box day before yesterday. Oh, Berry! I'm so glad we have a fire in our kitchen," she added solemnly, with a little shiver in remembrance of the dark, chilly cabin where she and her mother had remained in hiding for several days without warmth or light.

Mrs. Arnold gave Mollie a warm welcome, and when, late that afternoon, the little girl started for home, Lily, carrying a basket filled with food, went with her; and Berry promised to be at the brook, in the place where she and Mollie always planned to meet, by an early hour the next forenoon.

That evening Berry told her mother and father the story of the Braggs' wanderings, and of the hardships Mollie and her mother had suffered. "Wouldn't it be fine if Len could only come home and help them?" said Berry, as she finished the story.

"He may be here at any time, for his regiment is probably in Corinth," Mr. Arnold responded gravely. "I do not believe the Confederates mean to wait for Grant's army to attack them. The spies of General Johnston and

General Beauregard will keep them informed each day of the advance of General Buell's troops. Beauregard is used to winning; with the laurels of Fort Sumter and Manassas fresh in his mind he may decide to advance upon Grant's forces at once. Len Bragg is with Beauregard's army, and may find himself near home any day."

"That will be splendid!" Berry declared, smiling happily at the thought of the pleasure of Mollie and Mrs. Bragg if Len should suddenly appear.

But Mr. Arnold shook his head.

"Anything but that, Berry," he replied. "If Beauregard's army surprises the forces of Grant and Buell it might mean the capture of the Army of the Cumberland. The Confederate troops must be nearly equal in numbers to those of the Union forces. If Beauregard could take Grant by surprise it would indeed be a sad day for the Union cause."

Berry listened soberly. She well knew that her brother Francis was fighting for the cause of the Union that slavery might cease to exist and the United States remain an undivided nation. She now began to realize that war might come very near her cabin home; that General Grant's men, marching toward Corinth, might be surprised and captured by the daring and triumphant Beauregard. And that night Berry resolved to henceforth keep a sharp outlook for possible Confederate spies, or for any evidence of marching troops along the Corinth road.

"If I could let General Grant know that Confederates were on the march, then Beauregard could not surprise him," thought Berry, remembering that she knew all the forest trails and woodland roads, and that, if she kept a sharp watch, no body of soldiers could reach Pittsburg Landing, where her father believed Grant would land his soldiers, over either of the Corinth roads without her seeing them. "And no one can run faster than I can. I could get to the Union camp long before the Confederates, and then

General Grant would be ready," she thought, not realizing any of the dangers in store for such a messenger just before an impending battle.

"I'll go to the top of the ridge twice every day, and I'll make Lily promise to keep a sharp watch," resolved Berry.

At first the little girl thought she would tell her mother and father of her plan; but she remembered her father's caution in regard to keeping out of sight of wayfarers along the trails, and said to herself, "I'll wait until I have seen real soldiers. Perhaps until after I have seen General Grant himself. I guess my father will be proud if I run faster than any Confederate soldier." And so Berry confided her new resolve to no one but Lily; and the colored girl proved the best possible assistant.

98

CHAPTER XIV
ON GUARD

Mollie Bragg wondered a good deal about Lily. Berry treated the colored girl as if she had the same right to friendship and kindness as if her skin were white. In fact, to Mollie it sometimes seemed that Berry was more kind and thoughtful toward Lily than toward anyone else, and this sadly puzzled Mollie; and, one day when the two little friends were making a playhouse under the big oak tree behind the Arnold cabin, Mollie said:

"Berry, Lily's a nigger, ain' she?"

Berry, who was carefully building a "make-believe" fireplace, stopped and gazed at Mollie in astonishment.

"Why, Mollie! You know just as well as I do that Lily's a negro girl. My mother says Lily couldn't be any blacker!" she responded.

"Well, you treats her jes' like you treats white folks; you says 'please' to her when you asks her to do things, an' you says 'thank you' after she's done 'em. I've heard you, Berry," and Mollie nodded solemnly, as if expecting Berry would promptly deny it.

But Berry also nodded, and only looked more and more surprised.

"Of course I say 'please' and 'thank you,'" she said; "and of course I treat her just as I would a white girl. I guess I ought to treat her better than I do," Berry continued thoughtfully, "because she has never had anyone to be kind to her until she came to live with us. Lily can't help being black. Just suppose your skin was black, Mollie, you'd be Mollie just the same inside of your skin, wouldn't you?"

"Mebbe I would," Mollie replied soberly.

"And just think how many things Lily knows that we don't," Berry continued eagerly. "Don't you remember that wood pewee's nest she showed us between the forked twigs of the young oak tree near our gate?

and the cat-bird's nest in the cedar tree? and all the stories she tells us, Mollie. About the thrush that pounds acorns on the ground until the shells are broken and he can get the nut; and she made that beautiful basket; and—and——" Berry hesitated for a moment in her list of Lily's achievements and then said, "And, anyway, she is 'Lily,' and I like her just as well as if she were white."

Mollie nodded. She could understand Berry's final reason better than any other: to like Lily "Just because she is Lily" satisfied her.

"I likes you, Berry, jes' because you are Berry," she said; and the two little friends resumed their play. Neither of them imagined that Lily had heard every word of the conversation from her perch on one of the lower branches of the big oak tree. It was Lily's secret hiding-place. Perched there among the branches she could look far down the ravine in one direction, and toward Shiloh church in the other, and with little danger of being discovered. She had just settled herself there at the time when Berry and Mollie arrived beneath the tree, and so could not help hearing Mollie's questions and Berry's reply. And as she eagerly listened to Berry's declaration that she, Lily, knew many things that the little white girls did not know, that she was "just the same inside her skin" as if she were a white girl, and Berry's assertion of affection toward her, Lily nearly tumbled from the tree. Tears came to her eyes, and a new sense of happiness filled her heart. For the first time in her life the homeless, uncared for negro girl knew that she was loved. "Jes' like I was white," she whispered to herself. And her affection for Berry deepened, and she again made solemn vows that no harm should ever come near "Missie Berry."

It was the next day when Berry confided to Lily the news that Confederate troops might, at any day, appear on the Corinth road.

"That is, unless the Union soldiers march to Corinth first," explained Berry. "And, Lily, my brother Francis is a Union soldier; he's fighting to set you free!" she continued, her brown eyes resting solemnly upon Lily.

"Yas, Missie Berry. I reckon yo' brudder would do dat," Lily responded, "an' yo' don' wan' de Confedrits ter ketch de odder army? Yo' means ter watch out fer 'em?" questioned Lily.

"Yes, Lily, and you must help me. And it must be a secret. Not even Mollie Bragg is to know," cautioned Berry. "We must begin to-day," she added.

"Yas, Missie Berry," Lily promptly agreed. Whatever Berry wanted done Lily would do without question. But there was something on Lily's mind that troubled her. She knew that Berry made daily visits to the red-buds, ready to fulfil the promise to the "witch"; and Lily now resolved to tell her young mistress that the voice Berry had heard at midnight as the wind swept down the ridge had been the voice of the man of whom Berry seemed afraid. And now the colored girl began to wonder if this man might not be one of those Confederates for whom Berry meant to watch.

"Missie Berry, yo' knows w'ot I tells yo' 'bout de witch-tree? An' yo' 'members de night yo' wen' down dar, wid de win' a-howlin' an' a-screechin', an' de dark jes' lak' a black wall? I wus clus beside yo', Missie Berry! An' dat wan' no witch w'ot call yo' 'boy,' an' makes yo' promis' ter kerry a letter. No, Missie! 'Twas dat man we saw a-cookin' a burd ober der fire by de ledge!"

It was now Berry's turn to be surprised. But she instantly realized that Lily was right; and when Lily added, "I follered arter dat man an' I knows," Berry looked at her companion admiringly. "Lily!" she exclaimed, "my father thought that man was a spy; and probably the letter he means to hide at the witch-tree will be for some Confederate general."

"Do yo' reckons 'twill be fer sum Confedrit gen'ril?" questioned Lily.

"Yes; because he has been about Shiloh all winter, I'm sure he has; keeping watch of the Tennessee River, so that he could send word of Union troops being landed. And the time I met him at the brook I bragged of how fast I could run," Berry continued eagerly, "and that's what made him want me for a messenger. He must have been hiding near the brook, Lily, the day you told me about witches."

"Dat's so, Missie Berry! An' I reckon he got de cake an' de honey," Lily responded regretfully.

"He's exactly like the cupboard mouse that Mrs. Bragg told me about," Berry declared, remembering how difficult it had been for her to secure the cake, and how much trouble she had taken to please some possible witch, only to have the woodsman laugh at her folly.

"I ain' nebber heard no story 'bout de cupboard mouse," said Lily; and Berry repeated it, greatly to the negro girl's satisfaction.

"Dat am a fine story, Missie, an' maybe we's gwine ter set de cat af'er dis mouse dat kep' all de cake ter hisse'f," she chuckled.

Berry was sure that any message this wandering spy might leave at the red-bud tree, trusting to her promise to run her swiftest to deliver it to whomever it might be addressed, would be a message of great importance to both the contending armies. It might be to inform General Johnston of the progress of Grant's army, or it might even tell when it would be best for Johnston's troops to march toward Pittsburg Landing, thought Berry; and her brown cheeks flushed with excitement at the possibility that she, Berenice Arnold, a little Yankee girl from far-off Vermont, of whom General Grant had never heard, might do this great soldier a real service by delivering this message, whatever it might prove to be, into his hands.

"For the army that knows first what the other army plans to do will surely have the best chance," she gravely decided, and resolved that it should be through no fault of hers if the message did not promptly reach the commander of the Union forces.

Berry could now think of but little else than her plans to outwit the spy. She realized that henceforth a constant watch must be kept, that either Lily or herself must be steadily on the alert, so that the moment a message was deposited at the witch's tree she could start instantly for the race that she firmly believed might result in the triumph of the Union forces.

As all these thoughts went swiftly through her mind, Berry stood flushed and silent, while the negro girl watched her, wondering what her young missie was thinking about, and when at last Berry exclaimed: "Lily! Instead of standing here we ought to be on the outlook for that man," Lily nodded her head soberly and promptly agreed; and when her young mistress said that Lily must start at once for Shiloh church, carefully keeping out of sight of any possible traveler along the trails, Lily was quite ready to obey.

"And if you see any signs of him, or get a glimpse of him, hurry back as fast as you can and tell me," said Berry as Lily started off.

For a moment the negro girl hesitated; she knew that Mrs. Arnold would expect her to return to the cabin with Berry, and she remembered that there was work for her to attend to; beside this Lily was sure that, as she could not explain her absence, Mrs. Arnold would think she had purposely neglected her duties, and as Lily was always eager to win Mrs. Arnold's approval she now had to choose between being praised and approved by Mrs. Arnold for returning promptly, and so disappointing Berry, or obeying Berry's wish and having Mrs. Arnold think her a thoughtless and ungrateful girl. But her indecision lasted only a moment. Berry would always hold the first place in Lily's affections; to please Berry seemed the most important thing. Lily would never forget that it was Berry who had rescued her from the dangers and hardships of her perilous flight from slavery, and brought her to the safety and comfort of her own home; so Lily started off toward Shiloh church, going almost noiselessly along the rough path.

As Lily made her way up the slope she thought of all the trouble this woodsman spy was making.

"'Pears like 'tain' only dat he am a-botherin' ob Missie Berry, but he am a-stirrin' up trubble fer dat Gen'l Grant an' fer Missie Berry's brudder, an' dey's a-fightin' ter set me free; looks like I orter do somet'ing to dat spy to stop his doin's," she whispered to herself, and her thoughts flew to possible aid from "witches," but she shook her head remembering how they had failed her young mistress.

"Looks 's if I'd got to conjure up some way by myse'f," she decided, and before Lily reached the woods that bordered on the little clearing where stood the rough cabin-like structure known as Shiloh church, she had thought of several plans by which she could prevent this threatening stranger from being of further trouble either to Berry or Berry's brother, or to General Grant. But, notwithstanding the making of plans, Lily's eyes had been sharply on the alert for any noise that might indicate someone near at hand, and she had frequently stopped to listen for sounds of movements that would betray any traveler along those mountain trails. But beyond the bubbling song of the wood-thrush, the musical calls of the pewee and scarlet tanager, and now and then the rush through the underbrush of some small woodland creature, there was nothing to be heard, and a quick glance about the clearing proved that there was no lurking stranger in sight.

Close by where Lily had halted grew a bunch of slender ash saplings, and, after she had satisfied herself that there was no one within sight or hearing, Lily drew out the pocket-knife that Mr. Arnold had given her, and after carefully examining the size and condition of the various saplings, she began to cut at a branch of one of the larger trees. In a short time she was able to break the branch off without splitting it.

"Dat gwine ter make a good 'nuff bow," she decided, with a little chuckle, "an' I reckon I kin cut off de top of my moc'sin fer de cord, an' dar's some fine arrow-wood in dat shed back of de church." And Lily, still careful to keep out of sight of any possible traveler, slunk along the edge of the woods and came out behind the rough shed where Mr. Arnold kept a store of seasoned wood for repairs on the church.

It did not take long for her to find a number of slender pieces of hard wood of the desired length for arrows, and seating herself on an old stump behind the shed Lily began to whittle one of these into the proper shape, notching one end and pointing the other end.

"I reckon I won' mek but one arrow ter-day," she decided, as she pulled off one of her moccasins and with great care carefully cut two slender strips from its top. With these she proceeded to string the bough cut from the sapling, and although it lacked the force and rebound of seasoned wood, it nevertheless proved equal to speeding the arrow with considerable force.

"I jes' fin' a chanst ter mek dat spy t'ink he's shot," she thought, as she turned toward home, realizing that hours had passed since she had parted from Berry, and beginning to dread Mrs. Arnold's questionings as to her absence.

"I reckon I cyan't say nothin', jes' kind of act sulky," she decided mournfully; but a moment later she forgot her own troubles. The soft, even pad of approaching footfalls made her scurry into the underbrush and conceal herself, and she was not a moment too soon, for she had hardly crouched behind a thick growing mass of laurel, before the hated figure of the spy came into sight.

Lily held her breath until he had passed her hiding-place, then she stepped out noiselessly into the path behind him, drew her bow, took careful aim, and the clumsy arrow sped through the air striking the man sharply on his neck.

With a yell that echoed through the silent woods he gave a leap forward, and fled as if pursued by an army of foes. As, indeed, he for the moment believed himself to be. The impact of the sharp pointed arrow had left its mark on his neck, a bruise that he believed to be that of a glancing bullet, and he afterward wondered why he had not heard the report of the rifle, and finally decided that he had heard it. But he did not turn back or seek to discover his assailant, but Lily's clumsy arrow had made him resolve that there was no time to be lost in sending a message to Corinth, and as he crawled into a hiding-place that he believed secure he decided to take no more chances by traveling on trails.

If Orson could have seen the delighted Lily as she gazed after his fleeing figure, it is probable that she would have had to flee for her life, for Lily fairly danced with delight, and as she sped toward the cabin she would frequently come to a standstill and laugh and wave her bow in triumphant satisfaction. While she had not really injured the dreaded stranger Lily was sure that she had frightened him, and was well satisfied with that.

Meanwhile Berry had met Mollie at the brook, as they had agreed on, and the two friends turned toward the Arnolds' cabin. Although Berry's thoughts were full of the spy and the mysterious message, she realized that she must not speak of them to Mollie; and as she looked at Mollie's happy face, and noticed how much better the little girl looked since the day when Berry had discovered the returned wanderers in their own cabin, Berry for the time forgot her plans to help the Union Army and thought only of what she could do for this friend who depended so much on her.

"I am going to teach you after this, Mollie," she said, reaching out to clasp Mollie's hand firmly in her own as they walked on side by side. "You see, Father is too busy just now; and I am sure I can help you learn to write."

"Oh, yes! Why, you can teach me all you know!" Mollie agreed eagerly, thinking how fortunate she was to have such a friend.

"Perhaps so," responded Berry a little doubtfully. "Anyway I am sure I can teach you to write, and then if you ever go away again you can write me."

"I don't want to ever go away again," Mollie declared soberly, remembering the weeks of uncertain wanderings about the mountains during the past winter; weeks when she had often known cold and hunger and fear, and that made her rough cabin home seem a place of comfort and safety, and which she hoped never again to leave.

Clasping Berry's hand, and tightly holding her birthday doll, "Mis' Ellen Arnold," to which Mollie had clung during all her wanderings, Mollie listened happily to Berry's plan for teaching her to write, and to learn wonderful things, such as who discovered America, the places first settled, and of the great rebellion that had made America an independent nation.

Mrs. Arnold was standing at the cabin door as the two little girls came up the path, and smiled as she noticed how eagerly they were talking and how much better Mollie seemed. But where was Lily, she wondered, for there was no sign of Lily; and after greeting Mollie and telling Berry that she and Mollie could help themselves to a freshly baked ginger cake that was cooling on the kitchen table, she began to ask about the missing Lily.

"Where is Lily?" she questioned; and much to her surprise was obliged to repeat her question before Berry replied:

"Oh! Lily's coming."

So supposing the colored girl might appear at any moment, Mrs. Arnold did not question Berry further. Berry brought her slate to the porch steps, and began to show Mollie how to trace letters, and for a time no more was said in regard to Lily's absence. But as the hour of noon drew near and there was no sign of her, and when Mrs. Arnold had several times come to the cabin door and looked down the path in search of the missing girl, Berry began to feel uneasy. Suppose after all the stranger was in search of runaway slaves and had recognized Lily, she thought fearfully, and had captured the negro girl and taken her away! And Berry found it difficult to sit quietly beside Mollie on the porch step instead of rushing off to search for Lily.

Dinner-time came and as they gathered at the table Lily was still missing, and now Mrs. Arnold also began to feel anxious. She wondered if it might not be possible that Lily had tired of living with them; or, perhaps becoming frightened by the rumors of advancing armies, had again started on her wanderings, and she questioned Berry very closely as to probable reasons for Lily's absence, and finally said:

"After this Lily must remain in the cabin, or near at hand, unless I give her permission to go with you, Berry. Now that Mollie is once more at home you can have her for a companion, and will not need Lily with you so constantly."

Berry listened, hardly believing it possible that all her well-laid plans could be so overturned; for she knew that unless Lily could go and come without interference that she might easily fail to secure the spy's message in time for it to be of any use to General Grant; and as her mother turned back to the kitchen Berry ran after her.

"Oh, Mother! I'll do Lily's work. Please, please, do not say she must stay in!" Berry pleaded so earnestly that Mrs. Arnold looked at her wonderingly. But she shook her head.

"No, Berry, you have your own work to do. And nothing could do Lily more harm than to let her run wild. After this I mean to have her learn more about household work, so that when she leaves us she can find a good home."

Berry stared at her mother in amazement. "But Lily isn't going to leave us, ever! I promised she should always stay with me," she responded, nearly ready to cry at these new possibilities; if Lily could not run about, if she was to be kept indoors, Berry knew that she must give up her effort to defeat the spy.

If Mrs. Arnold wondered at her little daughter's excitement over her decision she did not speak of it. "We will always befriend Lily, my dear, you know that," she said. But Berry would not be satisfied with this promise.

"Mother! Say that Lily shall always, always, always stay with us," she urged. "I have told her over and over that she should; and, Mother, it will be dreadful if Lily cannot go and come as she wants to. Why, she will think that you are displeased with her."

"I am displeased with her," responded Mrs. Arnold. "She has neglected her work and is wandering about for her own pleasure. Look! There she comes!" And Berry turned to see Lily coming up the path, swinging the clumsy ash bow in one hand and smiling radiantly as if very well pleased with herself. Berry started to run to meet her, feeling sure that Lily had important news; but Mrs. Arnold quickly prevented this. "Stop, Berry! Go back to Mollie. I want to speak to Lily. You can see that I was quite right; she has been making a bow and arrows and playing about in the woods."

"Please, Mother, don't——" Berry began; but Mrs. Arnold only shook her head, and Berry had only time to wave a welcoming hand toward her faithful messenger before Lily reached the porch.

Lily at once realized that her fears in regard to Mrs. Arnold's disapproval were justified. She made no effort to explain her absence, but stood with bowed head and downcast eyes while Mrs. Arnold told her that all the work expected of her had been delayed, and added that henceforth she was not to go out of sight of the cabin without permission. Lily listened silently. When Mrs. Arnold had finished the colored girl dropped the weapon she had so cleverly made and turned diligently toward the work of the cabin. It was nightfall before she found an opportunity to tell Berry of her successful shot at the spy, and of his flight along the trail. But Berry was too anxious about the fact that Lily was no longer to be free to go and come to praise her for her clever shot; and poor Lily, who was quite willing to bear Mrs. Arnold's blame, hard as that might be, if Berry was only pleased, went about her usual duties with so solemn an air that Mrs. Arnold became sorry for the girl, and feared that she had been too severe with her.

It was toward sunset when Mollie started for home. It had been rather an unhappy day for the little girl, for, after Mrs. Arnold's decision in regard to Lily, Berry's interest in Mollie's lesson vanished; she became impatient with all Mollie's attempts to write, and all Mollie's efforts to please her were of no avail; nor did Berry notice the tears in Mollie's eyes as the little girl bade her good-bye.

"I'll write better to-morrow, Berry, I know I will," Mollie faltered, as clasping her shabby, beloved doll, she started to join Mrs. Arnold, who had offered to walk as far as the brook with her.

"I don't care how you write," Berry had carelessly responded, her eyes anxiously following Lily, and eager for Mollie to go that she might hear whatever Lily could tell her.

Mollie gave a little sob as she turned and followed Mrs. Arnold down the path. She decided that she must be so stupid that Berry no longer cared to teach her. It was the first time Berry had ever spoken unkindly to the little mountain girl. Mrs. Arnold was quick to notice Mollie's trouble and comforted the little girl by saying that Berry was anxious about Lily; and when she added, "I have a skirt for your mother in this package, Mollie," the little girl's eyes brightened happily; for Mollie's chief sorrow was that her mother had nothing for herself. Whatever Mollie had she was eager to share with her mother. Mrs. Arnold knew this, and it made her very tender toward the little girl.

CHAPTER XV
SOLDIERS ON SHILOH RIDGE

Berry had not realized that her words would hurt Mollie's sensitive nature; indeed she hardly remembered what she had said, for her thoughts were full of marching armies; of sleeping soldiers suddenly attacked by relentless foes; and of herself, as a swift-footed messenger, reaching the Union camp in time to warn and save them. She went about the cabin after her mother's departure repeating a verse from a poem she had learned that winter, a poem by Sir Walter Scott:

"'Down from the hill the maiden pass'd,

At the wild show of war aghast,—

O gay, yet fearful to behold,

Flashing with steel and rough with gold,

And bristled o'er with swords and spears,

With plumes and pennons waving fair,

Was that bright battle-front——'"

"My lan', Missie Berry!" exclaimed the admiring Lily, "does yo' reckon we's gwine ter see all dat?"

And at Lily's question Berry quickly remembered that she should be off to Shiloh and keep watch. The little girl realized from her father's anxious face, and from what he said of the probable advance of Confederate troops, that any hour might see them on the march.

"I don't know, Lily," she responded gravely, "but I'm sure we ought to keep watch all the time; and I'm going up the ridge now."

"I bin a projectin', Missie Berry, 'bout yo' Ma tellin' me to stay clus in dis cabin in de mawnin's. Co'rse I mus' min' her," said Lily, "so I jes' wonner if I hadn' better keep a watch out at night. Dar ain' no reason w'y dose sojers wouldn' come a-creepin' fru de woods at night!" And Lily rolled her eyes and nodded her head solemnly.

"Oh, Lily! Of course! I forgot all about nights!" Berry responded eagerly. "But how can you keep awake?"

"I reckon I kin," declared Lily.

"Well, we'll begin to keep a steady watch from to-day. I'll be on guard days and you can watch nights," said Berry. "If you hear or see anything, Lily, you must let me know as quickly as you can!"

"Yas, Missie Berry, I kin swarm up dat oak tree side yo' winder an' tells yo', if I hears sojers or sees armies," promised Lily, and returned to her work, while Berry put on her red cap and started off for another look along the roads leading to Corinth.

It was the twenty-eighth day of March, 1862, and on that very day General Halleck, of the Union army, had informed General Buell that Grant would attack the enemy "as soon as the roads are passable." It was to be a deliberate forward movement on Corinth from Pittsburg Landing, to be undertaken some days later; for the Union forces had no idea of the Confederates' plan to surprise them by an attack on Pittsburg Landing.

The river banks at the Landing rise eighty feet above the river, but are cloven by a series of ravines, through one of which runs the main road to Corinth. Beyond the crest of the acclivity stretches a rough tableland. On this plateau five divisions of General Grant's Army of West Tennessee were camped, feeling themselves absolutely secure from any hostile visit, and unsuspicious of any shock of battle, and little imagining that a small Yankee girl was to be the means of saving them from capture.

As Berry ran along through the forest she could hear the cheerful songs of cardinals and robins. Squirrels scolded at her as they clung to the trunks of the tall oaks; and the air was full of the springtime fragrance. The silver chain and whistle hung about her neck, and Berry gave them a little loving touch, thinking of the absent brother who had given them to her. As she came out on the high plateau and stood looking toward the Tennessee River there was no sound except the songs of birds and the chattering of squirrels to break the stillness. Berry's keen glance scanned the distant road, but there was no moving form to be seen. She turned and looked toward Shiloh woods; the woods where Confederate troops would lay on their arms on the night before the Battle of Shiloh were now quiet in the spring sunshine.

Berry perched herself on the stump of an old tree and began to wish that she had asked Mollie to be her companion.

"Mollie would not imagine why I wanted to climb up here; and we could play our old games," thought Berry, recalling the previous autumn when she and Mollie had made families of dolls out of sticks and twigs with moss for hair and with gowns of oak-leaves and vines. They had made playhouses among the ledges or at the roots of some big tree, where, happy and undisturbed, they would play for hours. Berry wondered if they would ever again play together on that pleasant hillside.

She had only been resting a few moments when she heard the crashing of underbrush on the slope beneath her. Berry quickly concealed herself behind a tree; and in a moment the sound of loud voices, the jingle of arms and the noise of approaching feet made her whisper, "Soldiers!" And it was not long before half a dozen men, in the blue uniform of the Northern army, came out into the open space on top of the ridge. They were evidently tired from their climb up the ravine, and, to Berry's surprise, they apparently had no notion of concealing themselves—they were talking and laughing together as if they had no thought of war.

Berry was near enough to the newcomers to see them distinctly, and to hear every word they said. She heard them speak of the army in camp at

Pittsburg Landing, and gave a little gasp of surprise, wondering if her father knew that Grant's troops were so near.

"There ought to be outposts stationed all along here," she heard one of the younger soldiers declare; and another laughingly responded, "Oh, Colonel Peabody, the Confederates won't march over these roads and gullies. It's the Union soldiers who will go after them at Corinth."

"That may be, but it would do no harm to guard the roads," responded the young officer gravely.

Berry waited to hear no more. It seemed to the little girl that there must be marching soldiers in every direction, and she crept noiselessly away into the shelter of the forest and ran toward home eager to tell her father of what she had seen and heard.

Half-way down the ravine she met her father, who was on his way home from a visit to the Braggs' cabin.

"Father! Father! There are soldiers at Shiloh church! I saw them! And Grant's army is at Pittsburg Landing!" Berry exclaimed, clasping her father's hand as if she expected an army instantly to seize him.

"Yes, my dear. And you must now stay closely at home. The main roads to Corinth will be guarded by soldiers; but our cabin is too far from the highways for us to see them," Mr. Arnold quietly replied.

"Do you suppose we will see General Grant?" asked Berry; and her father smiled down at the little girl's eager face.

"He will probably march on to Corinth in a few days," he responded, and then added, "The flare of his camp-fires can be seen from Shiloh; their outposts are not more than a mile from the main line. If the Confederates surprise them it will be a terrible struggle."

"But they mustn't surprise them!" the little girl exclaimed earnestly; and again resolved that she would watch more closely than ever for any sign of the approaching enemy.

When they reached the cabin Mrs. Arnold was on the outlook for them. She and Mr. Arnold spoke of Mollie and her mother, and Mrs. Arnold declared that Mrs. Bragg was sure that Len might appear any day.

"Their cabin is so far in from the highway that I think they will be safe," Mr. Arnold said thoughtfully. And both Berry and her mother understood that he was thinking that it might be possible, before many days passed, that Northern and Southern troops would meet in deadly conflict along those peaceful country roads.

That night Berry followed Lily when the colored girl started toward the barn. "Lily, I'm going to take turns watching at night!" she said. "General Grant's army is at Pittsburg Landing, and if the Confederates surprise them my father says they might capture the Union army."

Lily gazed at her young mistress a little fearfully. "My lan', Missie Berry! Yo' don' reckon we cud stop a army, does yo'?" she said, waving the milk pail as if it were a banner; "how does yo' reckon we gwine ter do sich a thing?"

"We can do it by letting General Grant know that the Confederates mean to attack his camp!" declared Berry.

"We shu' kin do dat, Missie Berry; pervided we sees 'um fust! I reckons we'll hev ter watch out sharp!" Lily responded soberly.

CHAPTER XVI

BERRY IS TAKEN PRISONER

Berry's morning lessons with her father were now for a time discontinued. The little household in the mountain cabin realized that the encampment of Union soldiers at Pittsburg Landing meant that a battle was near at hand; and Berry's thoughts, as well as those of her mother and father, were absorbed in what General Grant's next movement might be.

Mollie Bragg came nearly every morning to practise her lessons in writing, and apparently had quite forgotten Berry's thoughtless unkindness. Berry presented the slate and pencil to the little girl so that she might use it at home; and this gift made Mollie sure that Berry had not meant to be unkind. Mrs. Arnold had again fitted Mollie out with a neat dress of stout gingham. Mrs. Bragg had made the poor cabin neat and livable, and had planted the rough garden plot with early vegetables. Every day she and Mollie kept a sharp outlook for Len. But General Beauregard was doing his best to get his forces at Corinth ready for a march on the enemy and no absences were permitted. But Len was to see his mother and sister, nevertheless, much earlier than he then imagined.

Lily's first night of "guard duty," as Berry called it, passed without her seeing or hearing anything to awaken her fears. The colored girl, however, had slept for several hours as she crouched against a mossy log near Shiloh church. But Lily was sure that she would have awakened at the slightest sound. On her way home, in the gray light of the early morning, she had stopped at the red-buds and found a sealed letter under the rock at the roots of the tree.

"I reckons I'll let Missie Berry see dis fus'," she resolved, and followed Berry's plan of reaching her chamber by the help of the old oak; so that Berry was suddenly awakened, just at daybreak, by a gentle touch on her curly hair and a whispered word:

"Missie Berry, Missie Berry, de letter's cum," said Lily.

For a moment Berry believed herself dreaming, and rubbed her eyes sleepily. Then instantly she was wide awake, and seized the letter. It was enclosed in a brown paper, and tied with a coarse string. In the dim morning light Berry read: "For General Johnston, at Corinth," and beneath it in large letters, "RUN!"

The two girls stared at each other with sober faces.

"W'ot yo' gwine ter do, Missie Berry? Yo' gwine ter gib dis letter to yo' pa?" questioned Lily.

Berry shook her head. "I don't know yet. If I give it to Father I would have to tell him about my going to the witch-tree at midnight," she whispered. "I'll have to think what I will do." And Lily nodded and made her way noiselessly to the kitchen.

Berry turned the letter over in her hand. To open a letter addressed to another person did not occur to her. But this was a spy's letter; it must contain news of the Union army, secretly obtained, and Berry knew that it would be of value to the enemy and that it would be a service if she could give it to a Union officer.

"I'll carry it to the Pittsburg camp," she resolved.

The moment breakfast was over Berry sauntered out to the porch and instantly disappeared. She scrambled down the rough slope of the ravine, and followed a path just above the Corinth road. It was a day of early April, and a damp mist lay over the river and drifted in little clouds along the hills. Berry had to make her way with some caution, as recent rains had made the path boggy and uncertain; but within an hour she was in sight of the rows of white tents that dotted the rough plateau facing the Tennessee River. Not a single spadeful of earth had been thrown up for entrenchments; no horseman patrolled the encampment. As Berry stood for a moment looking at what seemed to her so wonderful a sight, she heard the sound of laughter, and a moment later a group of soldiers came from a tent very near to where she was standing.

"What's this?" exclaimed one of the men, as he discovered a slight boyish figure in a well-worn flannel blouse and knickerbockers, and wearing a red tam-o'-shanter cap, standing directly in front of him.

"Off with that cap, young man! Don't you know enough to salute the officers of your country's army?"

Berry instantly clutched at her cap, and bowed to each officer in turn.

The three men laughed again, and one of them, whom Berry now recognized as the officer she had seen a few days earlier at Shiloh, and who had been addressed as Colonel Peabody, exclaimed: "Pretty good for a Southern lad. What's your errand at this camp, my boy?"

"If you please, Colonel Peabody, I want to see General Grant!" Berry replied soberly.

"Sorry, young man, but the General is at his headquarters in Savannah, nine miles down the river! Did you call to ask him to dinner?" responded the officer, smiling kindly down at the brown eyes that rested on his with so serious an expression.

"No, sir; although I am sure we would be pleased to ask him to dinner," began Berry; but before she could continue, the officers, evidently greatly amused by her response, broke into laughter; and the man who had first spoken said, "Southern hospitality, eh? Well! This boy looks a bit different from most of those I've seen! What do you want?" he concluded a little suspiciously, looking at Berry so sharply that, for the first time, she began to feel a little afraid.

"This letter," and she pulled the brown-covered message from the pocket of her blouse, "I found it and I thought General Grant would like to see it," and Berry held the letter out toward Colonel Peabody.

"'To General Johnston at Corinth. RUN,'" he read the inscription aloud; and the three officers gazed at each other in amazement; and a second later Berry felt a firm hand grasp her shoulder.

"So you are a messenger for the Confederate spy, eh? Well, you have come to the wrong camp. What's your idea in bringing this letter here? Want to count our troops? Pretty clever scheme, wasn't it?" and the man turned to his companions, who nodded their agreement. They believed Berry had been sent to the camp to secure information for the Confederates, and that the letter had only been an excuse. Colonel Peabody thrust it into his pocket and, keeping a fast hold of Berry's shoulder, led her toward a near-by tent. "Guess we'll keep you with us until we march into Corinth," he said, giving her a little push into the tent, where two soldiers instantly sprang up from a small table.

"Keep your eyes on this boy until I come for him," commanded the officer, and Berry found herself alone facing the two soldiers, one of whom motioned to a wooden stool and said roughly, "Sit down!"

Berry quickly obeyed. This was a very different reception than the one she had imagined. She began to wish that she had followed Lily's suggestion and given the letter to her father. Once or twice she started to speak, but one of the men promptly commanded her to "Shut up!" with so rough a voice that Berry did not dare to continue.

She realized that she was a prisoner in the camp of the Union army, and that no one would know where to look for her.

"If I had only told Lily what I meant to do," she thought mournfully as the hours passed and her hope of a speedy release vanished. But she was resolved that in some way she must escape, and was on the alert for a possible chance to slip out of the tent. Once free from the camp she was sure she could outrun any pursuer.

The hour of noon came, and one of the soldiers sauntered out after his dinner. The other followed him to the entrance urging him to hurry. Berry was sure she would have no better opportunity to make an attempt to escape. In a moment she had slipped from the stool, and creeping behind the unsuspecting soldier, she gave him so sudden and unexpected a push that he stumbled, and she sped past him and was off, running her best toward the steep slope above which stood the camp.

With a yell the soldier was after her; and Berry dared not look backward. She was sure the whole army was in pursuit as she fled down the embankment.

124

CHAPTER XVII
THE EVENING BEFORE SHILOH

It was well on in the afternoon when Berry reached the cabin. As Mollie had not appeared that morning Mrs. Arnold supposed Berry was with her and had not been anxious. But Berry now told the story of her adventure, to which her mother and father listened in amazement.

"The soldiers did not give me a chance to tell them that I was a little Yankee girl," Berry concluded resentfully.

"No pickets on guard; and General Grant at Savannah!" exclaimed Mr. Arnold, quite forgetting Berry's experience with "witches" and spies, as Berry described the unguarded camp at Pittsburg Landing. "If Johnston and Beauregard discover these things they will attack at once!" he said thoughtfully.

"Perhaps that letter was to tell them," said Berry, adding: "I'm so hungry!"

Lily instantly sped to the pantry; and in a few moments Berry was happily occupied with a plate of corn bread and a pitcher of milk. Later on her mother talked seriously with the little girl, telling Berry of the possible accidents that might have befallen her, and no one at the cabin knowing where to look for her.

"And if you had given the letter to your father, my dear, he would have read it and discovered if it was of any importance," she concluded. Mrs. Arnold did not ask any promise from Berry, for she felt sure there would be no more midnight visits to the "witch-tree"; and she did not for a moment imagine that Berry had resolved to do "guard duty" for the camp at Pittsburg Landing.

A week passed, with heavy rains making the roads to Corinth nearly impassable, and convincing Berry that there was no need for anyone to look out for marching foes. But although Saturday morning, the fifth of April, dawned in a furious rain, Berry resolved it was again time for her to visit the distant ridge. But her father was ill that morning; Lily was kept busy at household tasks, and Mrs. Arnold required Berry's assistance, so it was not until night that Berry could leave the cabin.

Dark clouds were sweeping over the tops of the forest trees as the little girl lowered herself from the window of her room and made her way through the gathering darkness to the trail leading to Shiloh. Long before her journey was completed she heard strange sounds and muffled noises, but the rain had ceased and she went slowly forward, stopping now and then to listen, but with no idea that, in spite of rain and almost impassable roads, the Confederates had marched from Corinth, and that in Shiloh woods yonder, grimly awaiting the dawn, 40,000 Confederate troops lay waiting the command to attack Pittsburg Landing; an army that General Grant believed to be in Corinth, twenty miles away. This stealthily moving host now lay on its arms, weary from its day's march. No fires had been lighted; and sheltered in the shadowy forest a council of Confederate generals gathered in the small clearing toward which Berry was noiselessly approaching.

The flicker of a light attracted the little girl's attention, and she made her way toward it, and in a moment stopped suddenly, too amazed and frightened to comprehend that she was gazing upon one of the important scenes in the history of the Civil War.

Resting on a stump was a lantern; a drum served as a writing-desk; and seated on a blanket close by was General Hardee, broad-shouldered and muscular; General Bragg, who sat beside him, was wan and haggard; his iron gray beard and thin form in great contrast to that of Hardee's. Berry's eyes rested longest on a dignified and martial figure that paced slowly from the stump to the edge of the group. Tall, erect and powerful, with a gray military cloak thrown over his shoulders, General Albert Sidney Johnston, Commander of the Confederate forces at Shiloh, might well hold the attention of any observer; and Berry never forgot her only glimpse of this resolute and fearless soldier who, before another sunset, was fated to fall on the field of battle.

Walking quickly to and fro was a slender figure in gray uniform; the soldierly and handsome Beauregard; and Generals Breckinridge and Polk stood silent near by.

Berry, crouching behind a stump, could hear their entire conversation. She heard Beauregard declare that the Union camp was entirely unprepared to face an attack; that General Grant was nine miles down the river, and on the other shore at that; and, as he bade his companions good-night, he confidently announced, "Gentlemen, to-morrow night we sleep in the enemy's camp."

Berry waited to hear no more. Here was the very opportunity for which she had been waiting: to be of use to the cause for which Francis was fighting. She quite forgot her reception at the Union camp that morning of a week earlier as she realized how close at hand was the attack upon them. She knew that no time must be lost. The night was dark, and it would be no easy matter for her to find her way along trails and over the streams, swollen by recent rains, that she must cross to reach Pittsburg Landing. One clumsy step might plunge her down the ravine, or into the muddy waters of the stream; but she did not consider these things as she fearfully made her way from the steadily moving sentinels about the sleeping army. Alert as they were, they did not see or hear the little figure that slid from tree to tree in the forest darkness; and Berry was soon on a shadowy trail that would take her to the Corinth road leading to Pittsburg Landing.

Colonel Peabody, who commanded the first brigade of General Prentiss's division, had read the letter that Berry had given him; but, as he believed it some sort of a hoax, gave it little attention. Nevertheless he was vaguely uneasy that night of April fifth over the safety of the camp, and, long after his companions were asleep he paced about the plateau; and when a tired, panting little figure came running toward him out of the shadows he stopped in amazement. Before he could speak Berry was close beside him.

"I'm not a Southern boy; I'm a little Yankee girl from Vermont," she announced before the surprised officer could ask a question. "And there are thousands of Confederate soldiers in Shiloh woods who are going to march here early; perhaps they are coming now," Berry whispered, too tired to speak aloud. But she managed to answer the officer's sharp questions without faltering; and Colonel Peabody was quickly convinced that this tired little girl had brought news that might save the Pittsburg Landing camp from capture. He now realized that the little figure beside him could hardly stand upright, and lifting Berry in his arms he carried her to his tent and set her gently down on his bed. "Rest here, brave little Yankee," he said kindly. "You have indeed proved your courage."

Berry heard his words as if they were part of a dream; almost instantly her eyes closed. Before she awoke the battle of Shiloh had begun.

The morning of Sunday, April sixth, was already dawning as Colonel Peabody hastened to dispatch five companies of soldiers down the Corinth road. The divisions of McClernand, Prentiss and Sherman were at once ready for action, while Generals Hurlburt and Wallace made ready to defend the Landing. As the Union soldiers marched down the Corinth road they were met by a rattling fire of musketry. It was the advancing Confederates. Instantly the woods were alive with the yells of the exultant Confederates. The Union generals, overwhelmed by surprise, could only do their best to defend themselves. General Sherman's troops, with two batteries at Shiloh church, for a time held off the foe. Sherman himself held his surprised troops to their task, and was the chief figure on the Union side that day at Shiloh. General W. H. Wallace moved his troops forward to Sherman's assistance, but the Union troops were forced steadily back toward the Landing, and by afternoon the fate of the Union army was critical.

But at this crisis Nelson's division, sent forward from General Grant's headquarters, arrived, and rushed upon the scene. Darkness approached, and Beauregard called off his troops, confident that on the morrow they could complete their triumph.

Next morning, however, the astounded Confederates beheld a new enemy in the field: General Buell's troops and those of General Lew Wallace had arrived; and before Monday night the Confederate retreat had begun. It was conducted with masterly order and precision. The Confederates, winning the first day, were conquered only by the timely arrival of Buell's 25,000 fresh troops. But it is easy to picture the disappointment of the brave Beauregard as he led his men back to Corinth.

Berry had awakened to the roar of cannon, the reports of musketry, and the calls of officers urging their men forward. She peered from the tent door and wondered how she could ever again reach home. For the first time she began to think of how troubled and anxious her mother and father must be as they heard the reverberations of guns through the ravines, and realized that a battle was under way, and discovered that their little daughter was missing.

"But I couldn't help it," Berry whispered to herself, with a little sob. "I had to come." Her feet were nearly blistered, and she found it difficult to walk, and crept back to the bed. It was nearly dusk when a soldier stumbled into the tent, opened a box and muttered: "Here, the Colonel said to give you a bite to eat," and handed Berry some hard crackers and strips of dried beef.

"There's water in that jar," he said, pointing to a stone jar on a near-by table; and Berry drank thirstily.

"I want to go home!" she announced, turning toward where the soldier had stood; but he had vanished. Berry again found herself alone. The reports of artillery gradually ceased; darkness settled over the camp; and the little girl, who had brought the news of the advancing enemy, was apparently forgotten.

CHAPTER XVIII
AFTER THE BATTLE

Berry's absence from home on the morning of the battle of Shiloh made Mr. and Mrs. Arnold seriously anxious. The fact that Lily had also disappeared was of some comfort, however, for they knew the colored girl would do her best to protect and shield her young mistress from any danger. The position of the Arnolds' cabin in the remote ravine was, fortunately, out of range of the guns, and the terrible encounters between the Confederate and Union forces were all several miles beyond the ridge that sheltered the cabin. But Sunday, with the echoing sound of guns, passed slowly by to the nearly frantic parents. To venture far from the cabin was not to be considered; and, added to their anxiety for Berry, was the fear of what might have befallen Mrs. Bragg and Mollie. But at the approach of night the sound of musketry ceased, the roar of cannon died away for a time, and a heavy rain began to fall. But with darkness came a new sound: Union gunboats had come up the Tennessee River and began a steady fire upon the Confederates. Sleep was impossible, and when Monday morning came Mr. Arnold declared that he must go in search of Berry, and Mrs. Arnold determined to accompany him. But as they turned down the familiar trail, two miles from the cabin, to the brook, where Berry had met the spy, they could see the dense smoke from the guns rising in every direction; and down a near-by road a mass of Confederate soldiers in their gray uniforms dashed by.

"It is of no use to go any farther. We may be shot by stray bullets, or taken prisoners as 'suspicious' strangers," said Mr. Arnold. "Possibly some friendly officer has taken charge of Berry and Lily, and when the battle ends will send them safely home. All we can do is to return to the cabin and wait!"

Mrs. Arnold sadly agreed, and they made their way home, wondering anxiously as to the course of the battle.

"If the Union army had any warning at all of the advance of the Confederates they may be able to defend the Landing," said Mr. Arnold, as they again reached the cabin.

When Lily awakened on Sunday morning to the sound of echoing artillery, and when she discovered that Berry was not at home, she at once understood what had happened.

"Missie Berry's at de Union camp!" she promptly decided, "an' I'se gwine dar ter tek keer ob her," and Lily was off like the wind. But she found it no easy matter to reach her destination.

After she had left the rough ridge where the Arnolds' cabin stood and made her way down the ravine she was instantly in the midst of moving masses of Confederates; and it took all her alertness and caution to avoid discovery. For hours she crouched in thickets, and once even marched steadily along with a division of soldiers who were driving Union soldiers back toward the Landing; and darkness had begun to gather before the tired, frightened Lily reached the plateau above the Tennessee River, from where the thunder of guns held back the advancing Confederates.

Slowly and cautiously Lily crept along the embankment. Rain began to fall; darkness came; and the Confederates fell back; and the exhausted Lily crawled along and at last found herself near a tent.

"I reckon I'll jes' go in dar," she thought, "an' wait til' dis rain stops," and, making no more noise than a woodland rabbit, Lily softly crept under the swinging flap of the tent. But, quietly as she had entered, ears as sharp as her own, and eyes accustomed to shadowy woodland ways, had discovered her.

"Who's there?" called a familiar voice; and Lily jumped to her feet and ran forward.

"My lan'! Missie Berry!" she exclaimed. "Ain' I de lucky nigger ter cum right to dis tent! I'se bin all day a-gettin' har!"

"Oh, Lily!" For a moment Berry clung silently to the faithful girl who had braved every danger to reach her young mistress; and then quickly told the story of her discovery of the Confederates in Shiloh woods. "And now I want to go home. We'll start this minute!" she exclaimed eagerly.

"We cyan't, Missie Berry! Dar's milluns ob men a-fightin' out dar! An' lissen ter dat rain, Missie Berry! If we wusn't killed by guns we'd be droun'd daid! We shu' wu'd, Missie Berry. An' yo' ma and pa dey knows I'll tek keer ob yo'," Lily concluded, and Berry at last agreed not to attempt to start for home until the next morning. Lily curled up on the floor beside the cot where Berry lay; and, in spite of storm and the crashing sound of guns, the girls were soon fast asleep.

On Monday Lily was awake at an early hour, and left the camp to skirmish for food. It was too serious a moment in the great battle for Colonel Peabody to remember the little Yankee girl in his tent, but Lily managed to secure a quantity of hard biscuit and refilled the water jug. "We kin go home ter-night, I reckon," she assured Berry, who was now rested and eager to leave the tent.

Early that afternoon the sound of cheers echoed along the plateau, and Berry and Lily ventured to peer from the tent. A soldier rushed past them shouting: "Beauregard's men are retreating. The Battle of Shiloh is over!"

"Praise de Lawd!" said Lily; "an' I hopes dis ends de noise."

By four o'clock the last shot had been fired, and the Union generals found that in the two days' battle 15,000 Union soldiers had been killed or taken prisoners by the enemy, while the Confederate loss was not over 10,699 men.

In spite of Berry's pleading Lily resolutely refused to start for home until night.

"'Tain' safe, Missie Berry! Jes' wait!" she insisted; and Berry at last agreed.

It was six o'clock when the flap to the tent was drawn back and Colonel Peabody, his arm in a sling and a bandage about his head, stood smiling in the doorway.

"Thank heaven you are here, and safe!" he exclaimed, as Berry started toward him; and then, discovering Lily, dressed in Francis's old clothes, added, "Where did this boy come from?"

"From my home; it's Lily!" Berry explained. "She's going to take me home!"

The officer looked puzzled, but asked no further question in regard to Lily; and a moment later a soldier appeared with a pitcher of hot coffee, a plate of fried eggs and bacon, and another of biscuit. He set the food on a rough table and Colonel Peabody at once drew a stool toward it. He had hardly tasted food since the beginning of the battle, but he did not forget his visitors, and Berry was told to sit beside him, while Lily was given a liberal share. They were all too hungry to talk until they had satisfied their hunger, and Colonel Peabody was the first to speak.

"Now, little Yankee girl, tell me your name, or, better still, write it down for me. You will find some paper and a pencil in that box," and he pointed toward a wooden box at the head of the cot.

"Write your father's name also," he added, as Berry began to write.

"My brother Francis is a Union soldier. He's a Corporal!" Berry proudly announced, as she handed Colonel Peabody the paper on which she had written her own name and that of her father.

"Well, I think you should be a General!" declared the officer. "So your name is Berenice Arnold!" said Colonel Peabody, and in a thoughtful tone he repeated: "Berenice Arnold, the little Yankee girl of Shiloh," and then added: "If you had not reached us when you did with your warning of the advancing Confederates this camp would surely have been captured. General Grant will thank you himself."

"Missie Berry, I reckons we better be startin'," whispered Lily, and, before Berry could respond, Colonel Peabody rose to his feet and said:

"Before you go, Berenice, I must take you to the hero of the day, General William T. Sherman. His efforts led us to victory," and resting his hand on Berry's shoulder the wounded officer moved toward the door of the tent, with Lily close at his heels.

The Union generals were gathered in a tent near by discussing the fortunes of the day. General Rousseau, whose brigade had swept everything before it; General McCook and Crittenden, who, against tremendous odds, had held their stand at Shiloh church, and General Buell, whose arrival had given victory to the Union forces, were all gathered about General Sherman as Colonel Peabody with his two odd companions appeared in the open doorway of the tent. Very briefly he told the story of Berry's flight through the forest on the night before the Battle of Shiloh to bring the news of the stealthy advance of the enemy, and with a gentle push sent Berry toward the black-whiskered, grave-faced General whose keen eyes softened as they rested on the slender little figure; and, as he clasped Berry's hand and smiled down upon her, Berry wished with all her heart that there was some greater service she could do for the man who had that day won an undying fame.

Later on, when Berry attempted to repeat to her father and mother what General Sherman had said to her, she found that all she could remember was that he had called her "a brave little Yankee girl," and, when Colonel Peabody summoned a tall young soldier to go to the outskirts of the camp with the girls, that each one of the great generals had clasped her hand and smiled upon her and repeated General Sherman's words.

The late April twilight had begun to fade when Mr. and Mrs. Arnold from their seats on the cabin porch heard the sound of a clear whistle, three times repeated, Berry's signal, and started to their feet to see Berry, with Lily close behind her, running toward the cabin. And when the little girl told the story of her night watch in Shiloh woods, her journey to the Union camp, and all that had so quickly followed, her mother and father listened in amazement. There was no word of blame for the girl who had been intent only on being of service to the cause for which her brother was fighting.

"We have two soldiers in the family!" her father declared proudly, as she finished the story of her adventures.

"I tole Missie Berry yo'd know I'd tek keer ob her," said the smiling Lily, as Mrs. Arnold said to the faithful girl that she had been sure Lily had followed her young mistress.

"Len Bragg is at home," said Mr. Arnold; "he was wounded, but not seriously, in the fight along Corinth road, and carried to the cabin. I have just returned from there, and must go down again to-morrow morning."

CHAPTER XIX
GENERAL GRANT

The sunny April days brought many blossoms along the Tennessee ravines near Shiloh; trillium and butterwort, arbutus and violets were to be found, and masses of dogwood bloomed along the slopes, where only a few weeks earlier the fierce Battle of Shiloh had raged. The Union fleet had moved down the Tennessee; Beauregard, convinced that the campaign was lost, was about to leave Corinth in the possession of Grant's army, and it was felt that the Union cause would soon triumph.

In the Arnolds' cabin the little household had returned to the peaceful occupations of the days before the two armies had come so near to them. Berry's garden flourished; Lily was becoming a well-trained servant, and Mr. Arnold was rapidly gaining strength. Within two weeks after Beauregard's defeat Steve Bragg had appeared at his cabin, and was as warmly welcomed as if he had been a brave soldier returned from war. It was soon evident, however, that a change had come over Mr. Bragg, for he at once began to work steadily. He enlarged the garden; cut logs with which he built a shelter for the calf that Mr. Arnold gave him; made repairs on the old cabin, and was so praised by his wife and children for his industry that he firmly resolved that in the future no one should ever again truthfully speak of him as "Shiftless Steve." When he looked at his wounded soldier son Mr. Bragg also made many other excellent resolves.

It was late in May when Mr. Arnold made his first trip since the preceding autumn to Corinth, and brought back the long-hoped-for letter from Francis, who was with the Union forces in Virginia, and wrote that he was well. But it seemed to Berry that her father had other good news; he smiled so often, she noticed, and Berry had been quick to see that, whatever it was, her mother was in the secret.

"Maybe it is about going back to Vermont this summer," she decided, for Berry knew that her father and mother were both hopeful that a return to their New England home might soon be possible, and when Mrs. Arnold announced that she was going to have a party, Berry was convinced that she was right in her conclusions.

"Of course 'a party' means that we are to have the Bragg family to dinner," said Berry. But Mrs. Arnold shook her head smilingly.

"That's not what this party means. Although Len is so much better that we will ask them all to come up on next Sunday. This party is a surprise!" she responded.

"Tell me, Mother! Oh! Please tell me!" urged Berry, but Mrs. Arnold laughingly refused.

"No, my dear! Not until the very day comes. And then you are to wear your white muslin dress. I will let out the tucks and the seams so it will do, and your Roman sash, and be a real little Yankee girl. And Lily shall have a dress and a white apron and cap. And I shall wear my gray tibet dress, and your father will wear a white collar! Yes, indeed! It is to be a great occasion!" and Mrs. Arnold laughed again, as if her secret was one that meant a great pleasure near at hand.

So Berry was greatly puzzled, and she and Lily waited expectantly for the day to come when they would be told to discard knickerbockers and blouses and put on the dresses that were ready for them, and on the morning of June first, Berry awoke to find her mother taking the white muslin dress from the closet.

"Oh, Mother! Is to-day the party?" exclaimed the little girl, springing out of bed. "And who is it, Mother? Who is coming? You said you would tell me when the day came!" And Berry seized her mother's arm and looked pleadingly up at her mother's smiling face.

"Yes; as soon as you are dressed, dear!" responded Mrs. Arnold. "Put on your white stockings and slippers, and make these short curls as neat as you can!" and she touched Berry's brown hair, and left the room.

"Oh! How can I wait!" thought Berry impatiently as she hurried to dress. "If I was in Vermont I should think it was either the minister, or Aunt Melvina coming to visit," she decided, as she vigorously brushed her brown curls.

When Berry reached the kitchen she exclaimed in amazement, for the table was spread for six people. Its coarse cover was white as snow, and the blue of the dishes, the glass dish filled with wild strawberries, and the white bowl filled with violets, gave it a very festive air. Lily, in a blue dress, and wearing a white cap and apron, was busy at the stove, and Mrs. Arnold was just cutting out a pan of rolls, while Berry's father, "dressed for church," as the little girl exclaimed, stood in the open doorway over which hung the American flag.

"Who is it? Who is it that is coming? I should think it was General Grant himself!" exclaimed Berry as she ran toward her father.

Before Mrs. Arnold could speak and fulfil her promise there was the sound of hoofs, the jangle of harness, and Mr. Arnold ran down the path. Berry was close behind him, but she suddenly stopped short.

"It's Colonel Peabody!" she exclaimed, and then noticed a bearded man, mounted on a fine gray horse, whom her father was eagerly welcoming. Behind these two officers rode the young soldier, whom Berry instantly remembered as the one who had guided Lily and herself from the camp at Pittsburg Landing.

The two officers dismounted, and the young soldier took charge of their horses.

Berry stood on the path not knowing quite what to do, but Colonel Peabody came to meet her, and in a moment Berry was being led toward that quiet, unimposing, and unostentatious officer, Brigadier-General U. S. Grant; whom, in 1862, neither public opinion, nor his own thought, had marked out for the mighty achievements before him.

"HERE IS THE LITTLE MESSENGER OF WHOM I TOLD YOU."

As Berry heard Colonel Peabody say: "General Grant, here is the little messenger of whom I told you, the Yankee girl of Shiloh!" she looked up to meet the steady, friendly glance of the grave eyes of the great General of the Civil War, and it was Berry who walked beside him to the cabin door, and who sat at his right hand at that simple breakfast party where the war-worn soldiers feasted on hot rolls and coffee, and praised the broiled chicken and hominy that Mrs. Arnold and Lily had so carefully prepared.

The visit was a brief one; within an hour the "party" was over, and General Grant and his companions were again on horseback. As Berry bade them good-bye General Grant rested his hand lightly on the curly head, and said gravely:

"Good-bye, Berenice. Be sure I shall not forget you," and Berry smiled up at the serious face and responded:

"I wish I were a soldier, like my brother Francis, and could fight in your army, General Grant."

After the last sound of the horses' feet had died away, and Berry had ceased to exclaim over the "surprise," Mr. Arnold told the little girl more fully of the great honor that had befallen her.

"General Grant's visit was wholly for you, Berry," he said soberly. "Colonel Peabody told me of the plan on the day of my visit to Corinth. And you must not forget the honor of such a visit."

Berry nodded silently. Her thoughts drifted back to the night when in Shiloh woods she crouched listening to the words of the Confederate generals planning their attack on Grant's army.

"I never can forget it," she responded, and added quickly: "Nor the Battle of Shiloh, Father! Or anything that has happened this winter. But I do wish we could go home to Vermont."

"Well, my dear, that is just what we are going to do. General Grant has given us passes through the Union lines, and within a few weeks we will start," replied Mr. Arnold smilingly.

"Oh, Lor'! W'ot's gwine ter become ob me?" wailed a smothered voice close at hand, and Berry turned to find Lily, with her apron thrown over her head, swaying back and forth on the path.

"You will go with us, of course!" Berry declared, and Mr. Arnold promptly repeated her words: "'Of course,'" and instantly Lily was smiling radiantly.

But Mollie Bragg heard the news of Berry's departure with a sad heart. Not even the gifts that the Arnolds bestowed on Mollie's mother could comfort the little mountain girl for the loss of the only playmate she had ever known. The only comfort for Mollie was the fact that Berry promised to write to her, from far-off Vermont.

"And you can write to me, Mollie," Berry reminded her, and at this a smile crept over the little girl's face.

"Yes, I kin," she responded proudly. "Len says I'm a right smart writer."

"And sometime I'll come back and see you," Berry promised.

Mollie's pale eyes brightened. "Oh, Berry! I hopes you will come back," she said eagerly. "Promise you will." And again Berry promised. But it was many years before the little Yankee girl visited the cabin on the ridge beyond the battlefield of Shiloh, and fulfilled the promise to the little mountain girl.

www.ingramcontent.com/pod-product-compliance
Lightning Source LLC
Chambersburg PA
CBHW061219210726
48294CB00006B/1901